For Eleanor

A WEEKEND FOR LOVE

by

Glenna Finley

*One day we'll spend
a lifetime—as sweet as
that lovely weekend.*
—Moira-Heath

A SIGNET BOOK

NEW AMERICAN LIBRARY

PUBLISHER'S NOTE

This novel is a work of fiction. Names, characters, places, and incidents either are the product of the author's imagination or are used fictitiously, and any resemblance to actual persons, living or dead, events, or locales is entirely coincidental.

NAL BOOKS ARE AVAILABLE AT QUANTITY DISCOUNTS
WHEN USED TO PROMOTE PRODUCTS OR SERVICES.
FOR INFORMATION PLEASE WRITE TO PREMIUM MARKETING DIVISION,
NEW AMERICAN LIBRARY, 1633 BROADWAY,
NEW YORK, NEW YORK 10019.

SIGNET TRADEMARK REG. U.S. PAT. OFF. AND FOREIGN COUNTRIES
REGISTERED TRADEMARK—MARCA REGISTRADA
HECHO EN CHICAGO, U.S.A.

SIGNET, SIGNET CLASSIC, MENTOR, PLUME, MERIDIAN and NAL BOOKS
are published by New American Library,
1633 Broadway, New York, New York 10019

First Printing, June, 1984

1 2 3 4 5 6 7 8 9

PRINTED IN THE UNITED STATES OF AMERICA

Chapter One

The architecture of the Stratford Inn might have charmed Queen Victoria, but Gray Stanton's first look at the three-story purple structure looming over the crest of the hill made him shudder visibly. With its gingerbread furbelows and leaning chimneys, the place would have prompted Frank Lloyd Wright to search the Yellow Pages for a bulldozer, and Gray's reaction was along the same lines. So far as he could see, the inn's only redeeming feature was the young woman who was polishing a glass insert on the old-fashioned front door. The padded down jacket which she wore atop some shabby skintight slacks couldn't hide a figure that at any other time would have found him maneuvering to strike up an acquaintance.

But just then, in the rain which had been coming down steadily since he had gotten off the plane in Seattle three hours before, a pocket Venus cleaning woman couldn't keep him from wishing to God that he'd never let himself in for such a jaunt in the first place.

The weather wasn't any real surprise. Anytime he ventured north of the Mason-Dixon line in February, it made sense to pack a raincoat and a lined jacket. Which was precisely why he left Arizona as seldom as possible during the winter. Even then, he wouldn't have been facing a long weekend in the rain if his younger brother hadn't joined a burgeoning television company whose budgets were the most important part of its new productions. Scott had emphasized that point during a phone call the night before, saying, "I need your help on this, Gray. You'll be practically next door to the inn at Port Lathrop—and the Game Farm, too, when you're surveying your project."

"Yes, but I'm just going to be there for an afternoon," Gray had protested. "I'm scheduled to be back in Phoenix the next day."

"You don't have to be, do you?"

"Well, it's not a matter of life or death," Gray had admitted, "but I have some things planned."

"She can wait," Scott had said callously.

"Like hell . . ." Gray broke off to ask, "Since when have you turned clairvoyant?"

Scott's snort over the wire showed what he thought of such a question. "Look, chum—you owe me one. Remember when I phoned your redhead last month and said that you'd been called out of town because of an emergency?"

"She's not *my* redhead, but I appreciated it."

"And the weekend before that when you needed an excuse for that concert you'd been roped into?"

"All right, all right," Gray cut in irritably. "You don't have to make this a family saga." He frowned as he thought over the coming weekend and decided that a change in plans wasn't going to make any appreciable difference in his life.

"All you have to do is look over the inn. From what I hear, it should be great for our exterior shots. If it isn't, there are five or six other Victorian houses in Port Lathrop. Then, of course, there's the Game Farm."

"Why do I have to bother with it? Haven't you finalized your arrangements for that segment?"

"Certainly we have—as far as the animals go. It's the weather I'm worried about. How soggy is the place? If it's knee-deep in mud, there's no use sending up our crew three weeks from now."

"All you have to do is make a telephone call," Gray suggested.

"I want an unprejudiced opinion. There's a lot of my bank account riding on this pilot," Scott said.

"I don't know a damn thing about filming in the mud. Or anywhere else, for that matter."

"That's all right. At least your opinion is free— that makes you the pick of the litter this time."

"Thanks. I'll treasure the thought. Just don't forget— this puts us square."

"Uh-huh. When will I hear from you?"

"It won't take me long to tour the port facilities," Gray replied, thinking aloud. "And I haven't gotten around to making any actual appointments there, so I suppose I could do your errands first—if it's all that important."

"Would I be calling you if it weren't?"

"I'm not sure—no, never mind, don't start the whole story again. I'll take a look at the Stratford for you and call you tomorrow night."

"Okay, great." There was a barely perceptible pause before Scott added carelessly, "Where had you planned to stay?"

"At a hotel in Seattle. Why?"

"Well, I just thought that as long as you had to drive to the Game Farm too, you might as well stay at Port Lathrop instead. Sort of soak up the atmosphere."

"With damp sheets and antediluvian plumbing? No thanks. I've seen Victorian guest houses before. I'll case the place for you, but I'm damned if I'll get knocked out of shape from a medieval mattress."

"Sure. I understand. It wasn't important."

If Scott had argued the least bit, Gray would have held firm, but his younger brother's dispirited tone and quick capitulation were enough to make Gray say roughly, "Besides, it's too late now to be sure of getting accommodations."

"Probably you're right."

"Oh, hell! I'll see what happens when I get there," Gray promised, remembering how much of his brother's bank account was invested in the company. If a stiff neck was another result of the weekend, it wouldn't be the end of the world.

His virtuous feeling had lasted almost until he'd reached the outskirts of Port Lathrop. It had started wearing thin after a lukewarm lunch that was even worse than the plastic breakfast he'd been served on the airplane. It disappeared completely after he parked in front of the Stratford Inn and felt water surge over the top of his shoe when he got out of the car. He swore under his breath as he jumped onto the soggy parking strip and then walked slowly to the front gate.

He stood there, strongly tempted to get back in the car and head for the attractive-looking motel that he'd seen at the outskirts of town. Afterward, he could phone Scott and tell him that his plans had changed.

While he stood there, debating with his conscience, a door slammed and he looked up to see that the attractive cleaning woman or whatever she was had disappeared into the inn.

So much for Northwestern hospitality, Gray decided with annoyance. He was aware that he was being unreasonable, but he was also aware that the rain was starting to soak through his shoulders as well as his shoes.

There was no hope for it. He'd take a gander at the inside of the place and see about staying over. But only one night, he decided firmly. Taking the sagging wooden stairs two at a time, he was brought up short on the porch by a securely locked door.

It was even more annoying to find a thumbtacked card which said, "Doorbell out of order. Please use knocker."

Gray followed instructions, banging a brass knocker hard enough to rattle the wooden door on its hinges. As he waited for someone to come, he saw that water was still seeping down from the small stained-glass diamonds in the top of the door where the cleaning woman had been laboring. He wondered why she bothered, since the rising gusts of wind brought the rain onto the porch with increasing frequency. If it kept on, the whole entrance would be dripping. That thought prompted him to knock again, and he almost hit the young woman on the nose when she opened the door abruptly.

She stood facing him, an exasperated expression on her face. "Didn't you see the sign?" she asked, before he could lower his hand.

Gray's mouth parted and then closed again as he tried to keep his temper in check. First appearances were deceiving, he told himself. From a distance, with her pale, softly waving blond hair and even

features, the girl had looked like a Dresden piece—
the kind that was placed on a mantel so that it
wouldn't get broken. At close range, however, he
saw a firm chin and alert blue eyes that didn't have
anything of the limpid quality he'd perceived. Even
her voice possessed a crisp edge that belied its husky
timbre. In fact, he decided, with her padded jacket,
worn gabardine slacks, and cleaning rag clutched in
one hand, she looked more like a pint-sized terma-
gant than the shy hotel help he'd imagined.

"Look, you may have time to go off into these
brown studies, but I'm busy this afternoon," she told
him even more impatiently. Clearly unimpressed by
a six-foot stranger on the threshold, she went on
distinctly, so that there could be no possible mis-
understanding, "There's a sign on the gate—"

"You have more than your share of them, don't
you?"

His calm comment made her pause. "What are you
talking about?"

"The same thing you are." He gestured toward the
thumbtacked card. "I just read this sign."

"Maybe you missed the other one." Almost automatically, she used the cleaning rag to catch one of
the drips still on the stained glass. "It mentions that
we don't allow peddlers or solicitors. None of the
inns do in Port Lathrop."

"I'll try to remember." Gray hunched closer, to get
out of the wind that sprayed rain over his face. "Do
you have something against guests?"

"I beg your pardon?"

"I asked if you had something against guests," he
repeated, feeling that the dialogue had gone on long
enough. At this rate, he wouldn't have to worry

about a room with a bath—he'd already had one.

Her faint "Of course not" merely heightened his determination.

"In that case, we can save on your heat bill and have the rest of this discussion under cover." He put a hand at either side of her waist, lifting her up and putting her down again—three feet inside the front door. He kicked that shut behind them both.

"You have one almighty nerve!" Her chin went up as she surveyed him defiantly.

He unbuttoned his nylon raincoat and shrugged out of it. "I'm also wet. Unless you have more guests than you can handle, I'd suggest another hospitality angle."

"So you *are* selling something!" she exclaimed triumphantly. "I was right in the first place. I told you—we're not in the market."

"For the first and last time, I'm not selling—I'm trying to buy a room for the night. Is that against the law in this damned town, too?"

"Of course not." Her eyes narrowed. "Your name isn't Stanton, is it?"

"You make it sound like a crime. What in the devil *is* all this?"

"I suppose it doesn't make much sense." Almost resignedly, she went over to an ornate table at one side of the foyer and pulled out a worn ledger. "Your brother phoned and said you might be coming. That is if you're . . ."

"Gray Stanton," he confirmed, reaching for a desk pen which protruded from a piece of petrified wood and then pulling the canvas-backed book toward him so he could register. "Believe me, I'm not any happier about this than you are." He signed and replaced

the pen before tapping the side of his head signifi-
cantly with a lean finger. "The way things were
going, I was beginning to think you had more than
your share of rooms to let."

"That's really made my day," she told him dryly
as she watched him pull a small black memo book
from his coat pocket and consult it.

"Since you know my name, I gather that you must
be Mrs. Elder. Leo Elder's wife?" He tacked the last
on a trifle hesitantly as he noted that there wasn't any
wedding ring on her left hand.

She shook her head. "Not even a shirttail relation.
The Elders were called away late yesterday. A family emergency in the Midwest. They were pretty
desperate, so . . ." Still clutching the damp rag in one
hand, she gestured expansively.

Gray dodged the drops of water dislodged in the
process and frowned. "All you had to do was say the
place was closed and I would have made other plans,
Miss—er—"

Amusement flickered for an instant in her deep-
blue eyes. "Cosgrove. Kimberly Cosgrove." Even as
she said it, she wondered why on earth she'd been so
formal. But she was darned if she'd simper and tell
the tall man that she'd been Kim for twenty-three
years, with rare exceptions. Especially when she'd
been caught looking like an Albanian refugee. If she
hadn't inherited the Stratford Inn two years before,
she would have salved her pride by informing him
that the place *was* closed. That even if he was six feet
tall with thick dark-brown hair, she wasn't impressed.
Besides, he was probably married or securely attached
to a glamorous girlfriend. Men in their early thirties
who looked like Gray Stanton and wore nicely tai-

lored tweeds weren't walking around loose in the general scheme of things.

From the way he was frowning at his surroundings just then, it was clear that he hadn't spent many of those years doing things he didn't like. It was a pity that she hadn't been able to discourage his brother when he'd phoned earlier. Probably it was just as well to make that clear. "I did try to explain to Mr. Stanton—the *other* Mr. Stanton—when he called. He said it wouldn't bother you that we weren't really receiving guests."

"Why?"

Gray's terse question threw her momentarily. "What do you mean?"

"Why aren't you receiving guests?"

"Well, for one thing, the cook's—ah—taking some time off."

Gray's lips tightened at the news. It was getting better and better, he thought irritably. Scott was going to pay for this debacle one way or another.

His expression made Kim hurry on to say, "You needn't worry, though. None of the Stratford guests has ever starved."

"That's a comforting thought. I hope that my brother mentioned I'd only be here for one night. Probably you can confirm his scheduling for exterior shots before I leave."

Kim brought her hand up to chew nervously on her thumbnail and found herself clutching the damp cleaning rag like a security blanket. She looked around for somewhere to get rid of it, hoping that her reluctant guest hadn't noticed the maneuver. She managed to deposit the rag behind a wicker fern container and said in a businesslike way, "I'll do my best. There is a workman doing repairs, and a group of visiting tour people due tomorrow morning, but that shouldn't interfere too much . . ."

He cut in as her voice trailed off uncertainly. "I have plenty of time. Have you ever run this place by yourself before?"

She drew herself up to her full height of five feet three, saying with dignity, "I don't really see what that has to do with anything. Would you like to bring in your bags now? I'm sorry that there isn't anyone to help you with them—"

"It."

"I don't understand."

"Bag. Just one bag," he explained, sounding resigned. "I'm traveling light, since I don't intend to stay long."

"You've made that abundantly clear."

Her tart comment disconcerted him, but just for an instant. "Yes, er, well—perhaps I could see my room. I'll get my things later. There'll be plenty of time before dinner, I imagine. Especially if the cook's missing."

"I had planned on a salmon and leek gratin—" she began only to have him interrupt again.

"—before you lost your kitchen help. Never mind. I don't expect anything ambitious. That's a common failing with amateurs in kitchens. Just stick to basics."

She stared back at him gravely and then nodded. "You're probably right. If you're not too hungry, I'll give you a cheese omelet or maybe a frozen dinner. Whichever you'd rather."

They both sounded equally repugnant after his long trip, but Gray managed not to say so. He tossed a mental coin, debating a scorched omelet against a packaged main course, and decided it didn't really matter. "I'll leave it to you," he said, trying to sound polite. He looked around the vast entryway, noting that drafts around the edge of the warped front door were making the fern fronds move. The inn's heating bill must be astronomical, he thought. And then as he saw his landlady shiver and pull her jacket tighter, he altered his thinking. It *would* cost a king's ransom if they turned up the thermostat—which must be sitting at rock-bottom for the moment. He could only hope they had plenty of blankets for his bed.

"Which way do I go?"

His brusque query startled her. "I beg your pardon?"

"The room. I'd like to see it. Now."

He'd turned toward the winding stair which took up most of the foyer and had his foot on the first step before Kim came to her senses. "Just a minute." As he frowned over his shoulder, she went on hurriedly, "Your room's downstairs. That is, if you don't mind. You'll be away from the construction—all the hammering and commotion."

His frown eased as her words registered. "Okay. Lead on, then."

"The stair to the base—" She broke off in the middle of her word and substituted, "—to the lower level is over here by the kitchen." Leading the way quickly past those darkened double doors, she switched on a light to reveal a wide stairway leading down.

"What else is down here?" Gray asked, noting closed doors as they reached a lower hallway.

"Just the laundry—but that's closed," she assured him. "And linen storage mostly."

She went on toward the end of the hall, hesitated

before two doors at the left, and then opened the last one. "This should be in order," she said, trying to sound calm but crossing her fingers as she entered the room.

Whatever he had been expecting, he'd been totally unfair to the Stratford's interior decorator. Gray realized that as he let out his breath in a soft whistle on viewing his surroundings.

"It's nice, isn't it?" Kim said, absurdly pleased that he liked something at last.

"Very nice." Gray walked slowly across the room, his glance taking in the understated comfort and elegance. A big antique brass bed held the focal point—its imposing headboard against the natural brick which had been used for the walls of the room. The bed comforter and dust ruffle were of a cheerful olive-and-white print, repeated in the drapes at either side of the glass doors on another wall. He made his way across the darker-green rug to peer out through the doors onto a tiny garden patio where a black lion's head lavabo could be seen on the enclosing brick privacy wall. There was just enough room on the patio for two lounges so that guests could sun themselves during the summer weather.

"That leads out to the street," Kim told him, indicating a thick carved door in the garden wall. "You won't have to come through the upper part of the house if you don't want to. I'll turn on these heaters." She bent down to flick on an electric baseboard fixture in the bedroom and in an adjoining bath, which carried through the brass decor with dark-red color accents.

Gray followed her to say, "I'm glad they didn't feel it was necessary to go Victorian in the plumbing."

"Even antique buffs draw the line at leaky faucets and no hot water. Or so Valerie tells me," Kim added hastily.

"Valerie?"

"Val Elder—Leo's wife. They share the management. Val did most of the decorating here, too."

"She's good at it. I might as well go out through the patio to get my bag and the rest of my stuff. It looks as if the rain has let up for a minute. Unless there's something else?"

As he paused, Kim's pale cheeks flushed and she reached quickly for the hall doorknob. "No, that's everything. We try to keep the garden door closed— you'll find the key in the lock. Dinner's at six, and there's complimentary sherry at five-thirty."

"I'll be up around six," he said.

His prompt answer showed all too clearly that he wasn't impressed by complimentary sherry. Kim's cheeks flushed again, and then the humor of the situation won. "I understand," she told him solemnly, "but you don't have to worry. There are lots of potted plants and ferns around if you don't like the label." She hovered on the threshold after opening his door partway. "I'm expecting some travel agents a little later, but I won't bring them down to this level, so you won't be bothered."

The door closed behind her, and Gray stared at it bleakly, deciding that the slanging honors were about even. He hadn't been diplomatic about that complimentary sherry. On the other hand, his new landlady hadn't bothered with kid gloves in suggesting that he stay out of sight until dinnertime. "The hell with it," he told himself firmly and turned up his coat collar before going out to his car by way of the garden gate to get his things.

He was putting his map of the peninsula into the glove compartment some time later when he noticed three men going up the front steps of the inn to knock on the door. Gray kept his head down as he sat in the front seat of the car, but when Kimberly Cosgrove let them in he was able to see that she had managed a quick change. Her cleaner's outfit had been replaced by a clinging jersey dress of a burgundy hue, the deep jewel tone providing a dramatic contrast with her blond hair and pale complexion. The pleated skirt which whirled around her knees drew his attention to a noteworthy pair of legs and ankles.

Gray's eyes narrowed contemplatively; even if Miss Cosgrove had been looking like a rummage-sale reject when they'd met, he probably had been a little off-hand in his manner. Of course, if she had bothered to exhibit any of the charm she was dispensing to those damned travel agents, things might have been different. Even from his distance it was obvious that the Stratford was going to be at the top of their list. The last member of the group was so dazzled by her smile that he tripped over the threshold going in.

Gray slammed the glove compartment closed once the group had disappeared into the house. He was tempted to go back in through the front door and make himself at home on one of those Victorian settees he'd seen flanking the fireplace in the living room, but then shook his head ruefully. Damned if he wasn't acting like a child over the whole stupid business!

He slid behind the steering wheel and put his key in the ignition. Instead of wasting his time, he'd better find a public telephone downtown and set up some business appointments. It was still a toss-up between several Northwest cities for his company's export site. Port Lathrop, with its location adjacent to the Strait and good rail connections from the south, might very well be the best of the lot for handling cargo.

Pulling up in front of a restaurant in the middle of town a few minutes later, Gray decided to call his brother after he'd had a cup of coffee and announce to Scott that he was on the scene. That way, he wouldn't have to worry about being diplomatic over the phone on the reception table at the inn.

Unfortunately, Scott wasn't in his office when the call went through and Gray had to leave word with his secretary that he was at the Stratford and would try to get in touch with his brother later on.

"He'll be out of town tomorrow and the next day, checking a filming location north of San Francisco," Scott's secretary replied. "And I'm not sure that he'll be back to the office this afternoon."

"It isn't a matter of life and death," Gray said, trying to reassure her. "Just put a note on his desk. I'll find him at the weekend if not before."

After hanging up, he looked at his watch and decided to try and make an appointment with the head of the port authority in town. He had a little more success on that call—the man telling him that he expected to be in his office for the next half hour and that he was just a few blocks away.

Gray swallowed his now-cooled coffee at the counter and informed the attractive young waitress that he didn't want a refill. "I'll come back again when I have more time," he said with a smile as he

paid his bill. Then, remembering the missing cook at
the Stratford, he asked casually, "Do you serve
dinner?"

The brunette looked crestfallen as she had to admit
that the restaurant didn't. "We're just open until
five," she said. "The only things in Port Lathrop that
swing at night are some canary perches—especially at
this time of year. In summer, it's better."

"I'll remember." Gray left a sizable tip beside his
cup and headed for his car, unaware that the waitress
stared woefully after him.

The port director's office wasn't hard to find, and
ten minutes later Gray was ushered into a modest
room whose main attraction was the magnificent view
over the blue waters of the Strait of Juan de Fuca.

A gray-haired man behind a cluttered desk smiled
as he stood to shake hands. He wore a salt-and-
pepper tweed suit with a white shirt and a conservative striped tie. He looked as if he subscribed to a
weekly news magazine, grew prize dahlias, and pa-
tronized a barber who'd never heard of a styling
comb. "I'm John Amherst," he said briskly. "Sorry
to have to hurry you, Mr. Stanton, but this other
appointment of mine won't keep. You can put me in
the picture of what your company needs and we can
go over the facilities later—if that's convenient for
you."

"Of course." Gray looked thoughtful. "The tempo
here at Port Lathrop is a little busier than I expected—at
least on the business scene. That's a good sign,
though."

"It's encouraging." Amherst's tone held a touch of
amusement. "The town fathers are trying to raise
money any way they can. I'm on the tourist board,

and we're starting a publicity drive on our Victoriana row next month."

"You mean those big houses up along the bluff?"

"Have you seen them?" Amherst asked, sounding pleased.

"More than that. I'm staying at the Stratford."

"Fine—fine. You'll like the Elders, who manage the place. They're a nice couple."

"They've been called out of town. Miss Cosgrove seems to be running things just now."

"Kim? I didn't know she was back."

Gray's dark eyebrows drew together. "I had the impression that she was a permanent resident of Port Lathrop."

"Oh, she was born here. Her grandfather was one of the early settlers, but Kim's been working in the East." A frown marred Amherst's pleasant expression momentarily as he added, "I hope that the fact she's home doesn't mean anything . . ." His voice trailed off as he visibly had second thoughts about that topic. "Anyhow, you should be comfortable at the Stratford while you're here. Get Kim to tell you the history of the place—it's well worth hearing."

"I'm sure it is . . ."

"But that's not the reason you came to town, is it?" the man finished for him. "We can get down to your business in the morning. By then, I should have some facts and figures about our port facilities that are bound to impress you."

"I'll look forward to it." Gray saw him give a surreptitious glance at his watch and stood up. "I won't keep you any longer now or you'll be late for your appointment."

Once he was out at the curb again and getting in

his car, Gray's mouth tightened in annoyance, wondering what he was supposed to do for the rest of the afternoon until he could legitimately appear upstairs at the inn. If he were staying any place but that hallowed historical monument, he could relax in his room and watch television or listen to the radio until it was time for a drink before dinner.

But rooms at the Stratford weren't furnished with modern-day amenities. Which left only the paperback he'd tossed in his suitcase. Of course, he could wander around the perimeter of the port area, but it would be more appropriate to wait for an official tour with John Amherst.

Maybe by then, the weather will have improved, he thought irritably as he drove through Port Lathrop's almost deserted downtown area. He couldn't blame the residents for staying indoors on such a foul day. The wind was gusting for a storm over the waters of the Strait, and the small ferry plying its run to the nearest San Juan island was wallowing in the swells and whitecaps. When coupled with a determined drizzle that seemed to soak through everything he was wearing, it wasn't surprising that Gray pulled up at the side of the inn in a frame of mind that matched the weather.

He went in through his patio entrance and tried not to notice how the puddle of rainwater was building up at the threshold of the outer door. One of those thick bath towels might have to be used as a temporary dike if the storm continued, so he'd better mention the danger to the elusive Miss Cosgrove at dinner.

Gray hung his raincoat in the small closet next to a brass washstand and turned on the hot-water faucet.

The water was distinctly tepid, and the temperature didn't improve as it continued to run. Apparently shaving in lukewarm water could be added to the list of Victorian amenities.

Gray walked over and turned up the wall thermostat. There was an immediate clicking and hum, which meant that at least he could dry his belongings and read his book in comparative comfort.

He left his damp shoes at a judicious distance from the baseboard heater and draped his sport coat over the back of a chair nearby. Then, pushing aside the padded spread, he stretched out on the double bed, grimacing as his feet came up against the footboard. It was all very well to furnish with tasteful antiques, but it wouldn't hurt to cater to a few six-foot males in the process. He slid around to the diagonal and stretched at full length. At least the mattress was all right and the pillows seemed okay.

He debated reaching over to turn on a lamp on the bed table and then decided against it. It had been a long day—what with getting out to the airport early and then the drive from Seattle after his flight. It wouldn't hurt to close his eyes just for a minute or two and get a little rest.

He settled into the pillow and yawned, deciding sleepily that maybe he'd been too hard on his landlady. There might not be much heat on the premises, but the bed was damned comfortable. He'd have to mention it when he finally surfaced upstairs for dinner, he thought, and fell soundly asleep while congratulating himself on such magnanimity.

Chapter Two

At that moment, it wouldn't have improved Kim's frame of mind to know that a partial accolade was in store from her star boarder. "And, thank God, the only one," she murmured to herself as she sat disconsolately on a stool in the Stratford's big kitchen. Gray Stanton had been in her mind all afternoon despite the way she'd banished him from sight. And that maneuver had been strictly a defensive one. Everything about the man—from his clothes to his manner—was geared to modern living. She didn't need to consult a hotelkeeper's guide to know that Madison Avenue types and Victoriana didn't mix. If only the Elders hadn't agreed to Scott Stanton's television-film request in the first place!

She leaned an elbow on the kitchen counter and stared blindly at the open cookbook in front of her. To be fair, she shouldn't be blaming the Elders for the television commitment; it had been a slow winter and the chance of unexpected revenue was too good to turn down.

All the time she'd been ushering those travel agents through the Stratford and outlining her hopes for the future, she'd been thinking how to change Gray Stanton's mind about her lovely old Victorian albatross.

By the time she'd served some coffee to the agents and waved them off, she'd decided to bring out the really good champagne for the cocktail hour and then astound Gray with a magnificent dinner that would leave him dazed with delight.

At least it would replace the cynical, thoroughly bored expression he'd had on his face when she saw him return to the inn. That observation came about because she was waiting for some water to boil on the stove and staring out at the rain-soaked street in the interim. She'd stood carefully back from the window when Gray had arrived so that he wouldn't add a nosy landlady to the rest of the inn's faults.

During her recipe searching later, she realized she must have forgotten to turn on the stove burner, because the teakettle certainly hadn't whistled. She walked over to switch it on and then drew a sharp breath when she saw that the teakettle was still full of cold water although the switch was turned to high. "Oh, no!" she moaned softly and glanced at the electric clock on the wall to confirm her fears.

As she suspected, the second hand was motionless. Consulting her wristwatch, she discovered that the electricity had been off for a good fifteen minutes. And probably would be off and on at intervals during the night if the wind continued gusting—she knew from experience.

So much for her hopes of a gourmet dinner! It was more apt to be hot dogs broiled in the fireplace if the storm kept up. And food wasn't the only problem. It was a wonder that Gray hadn't come storming up before this to complain about the lack of heat and lights in his room.

As Kim walked by the kitchen window, she noticed a streetlight flickering and discovered that the electricity was back on again for the moment. She'd have to provide a quick dinner if the spurt of power stayed on long enough and then suggest that her guest go to bed early.

Gray was unaware of all the planning over his head when he awoke after his refreshing nap. He stretched luxuriously and got to his feet. Time for a good hot shower, he thought as he headed for the bathroom to clean up. Strange how chilled he felt when there was heat coming from the baseboard installation. "I must be getting old," he decided, taking off his shirt and surveying his reflection in the bathroom mirror.

Fortunately he didn't seem to have aged perceptibly in the last few hours, and by the time he'd finished a brief shower and dressed, food was the main thought in his mind.

When he reached the top of the stairs and saw his landlady tending a cheerful blaze in the living-room fireplace, his eyes widened.

She'd been worth a second look before, but seeing her in a quilted coral velvet hostess skirt with a clinging V-necked cashmere sweater pulled him up short. As she knelt to tend the fire, the flames emphasized the purity of her features and brought gleaming highlights to the pale-blond hair. Like a Nordic princess, Gray thought, and then shook his head at such a fanciful streak. Good Lord! The Victorian atmosphere must be eroding his senses, he told himself as he walked into the room.

His appearance made Kim straighten abruptly, and she barely avoided tripping on her bouffant skirt in the process. "I didn't hear you coming up the stairs."

She took a deep breath to steady her voice as she went across to a tray on the mahogany table under the heavily draped window. The sight of the shrouded window gave her a twinge of guilt too, because she'd been intent on hiding evidence of the storm still raging outside as well as trying to preserve the last vestige of heat in the room. For the moment, the electricity was on, and she was wondering how brief she could make the cocktail hour so that she could manage hot food before the power dipped again. Her hand hovered over the iced champagne and then settled over the bottle next to it on the tray. "I hope you like sherry," she said, trying to infuse the proper amount of enthusiasm in her voice.

Gray hesitated, torn between the truth, which was "Not if there's a choice," and diplomacy—finally settling for the latter. "That'll be fine," he said, going over to stand in front of the fire. "What's the weather like outside?"

"Still raining," Kim said, using both hands to keep from spilling the sherry as she managed to hand the glass to him. That would be all she needed, she thought, giving his tweed sport coat and well-fitting gray flannels a careful berth. It was ridiculous that she should suddenly become so shaky—especially when she was doing her best to give an impression of calm, cool sophistication. If *only* she could offer him something decent for dinner!

She reached for her own glass of sherry and took a much bigger swallow than she'd intended.

"Here—let me help you." Gray took away her glass and slapped her between the shoulder blades, finally lifting her face up for frowning inspection. "Are you all right?"

"Fine," she got out in a strangled voice, trying to wipe her streaming eyes with the back of her hand. "It went down the wrong throat—or something."

"You *have* tried sherry before?"

She was reaching for a handkerchief in the pocket of her skirt and missed his slow smile. "Of course I have. Want to see my driver's license?"

"It might not be a bad idea. Oh, not that I doubt your word," he added hastily when she gave him a sudden frown. "I'm just a little curious about the setup here. My brother didn't fill me in on the details."

"I'm sure that the Elders gave him all the information he asked for."

He waved that aside and put his sherry glass on the mantel of the fireplace before he stared down into the flames, unconsciously holding his hands out to their warmth. "I wasn't thinking so much about the vital statistics of the inn—to be frank, I was wondering more about yours."

His dark-eyed glance was almost strong enough to cover her embarrassment over the sherry debacle, but she was careful to keep her voice casual. "It's amazing what you can find in small towns these days."

"Isn't it?" he confirmed dryly. "Do you intend to spend the rest of your life in this Victorian backwater? Most women your age have other ideas."

"Is that a personal survey or an educated guess?"

"I'm sorry if I sounded intrusive," Gray said in a tight voice, wishing that he'd stayed on a discussion of the weather.

"Not at all," she assured him and put her half-empty sherry glass back on the tray, wondering how she could change the subject to food. From the way the wind sounded outside, the electricity would probably be off again any moment. She decided suddenly to lay the facts out and satisfy his curiosity once and for all. "Actually I inherited the inn a couple years ago from an uncle of mine." Her lips curved in a wry grin. "Everybody said the same thing that you're saying—I should get rid of it at the earliest opportunity. Except that I like the old place and Leo and Val Elder wanted to try their hand at turning it into a moneymaker."

"I see." His eyes narrowed thoughtfully as he surveyed her.

Kim's laugh broke the silence before it could lengthen. "No, you don't. I'll fill in the rest of the spaces for you. You wouldn't believe how much it costs to keep a roof over your head in this place— even with solid bookings all during the summer. But we're close to turning a profit, and the Elders thought that a little television revenue wouldn't hurt at all. That's why they said yes to your brother, and that's why I hope your report won't be too negative, because I've already allocated the money we're going to get from him. It'll pay the carpenter who'll be coming at the crack of dawn to fix a leak in that same darned roof."

"You've convinced me." Gray held up his palm as if taking an oath. "I'll tell Scott that this is the place he's looking for." He paused then and grinned. "Is it all right if I suggest that he wait until the rain stops?"

"The way things are going, that might not be until the middle of summer." Kim pulled aside a drape to peer out onto the darkened street. "It certainly isn't any better. I think we'd better eat before the electricity goes again. Does an omelet sound all right to you?"

Gray manfully refrained from saying that a steak sounded a hell of a lot better. "If you'd like, we could go out to eat," he said, trying to sound impartial.

Kim shook her head. "That's no good. If the power goes, the whole town will be down. I'm sorry about this. . . ."

"It isn't your fault. You can't be blamed for a missing cook or the weather."

Kim started to say that if the power hadn't been out for a good part of the afternoon, she could have done better, and then decided against apologies. What was the old adage? Never complain and never explain. She'd already done more than her share of the latter. It was time to head for the kitchen or even an omelet might be impossible. "If you'd like to sit here by the fire, I'll get the food," she began.

"I'm not completely helpless in a kitchen," he told her. "Lead on and I'll follow. Here—I'll carry that for you." He took the tray with the used glasses from her and jerked his head for her to go ahead.

Kim managed a faint smile and nodded, hoping that she could keep a safe distance from him. Her skin throbbed just from the merest brush of his fingers when he'd taken the tray from her. Probably her cheeks were flaming, too, and she hastily put up her palms to cool them.

"Anything wrong?" Gray was close behind as she pushed through the swinging kitchen door and had to fumble for the light.

"No—no, of course not. You can put that tray over there by the liquor cabinet," she said, trying to sound brisk as she pulled an apron from a hook and tied it. "One omelet coming up."

Gray was looking with keen interest at the late-model commercial range and stainless-steel sinks against the wall. "This conversion must have cost a fortune. Is there a big enough payoff on food to warrant it?"

"Not really," Kim told him as she unearthed a small frying pan and a bowl in which to beat the eggs. "On the other hand, our customers don't want to drive a couple of miles for their coffee in the morning." She pulled a carton of eggs out of the refrigerator as she added, "Actually, it's no trouble getting customers for our dining room during the season, but it's a lot of work keeping a reliable staff. We don't have much to offer the college kids."

Gray had found a stool nearby and moved a pile of clean tablecloths so he could sit down. "You can't be far from that age group yourself."

She shot him a wry look as she rummaged for a whisk. "I'm twenty-three, going on sixty-five when I think of the bank loan we're trying to negotiate. Even if directors of a bank are people who have known you for years—like Mr. Amherst—they're still awfully conservative."

"John Amherst?"

She looked up to stare at his quiet figure on the stool. "Why, yes. He's an old friend of my father's. Do you know him?"

"We met today," Gray said briefly. "I thought he was port director here."

"He is, but he is also one of the bank directors—in charge of construction loans. The Elders made an appointment for him to inspect the inn this afternoon, but he couldn't make it. I hope he can come tomorrow—otherwise I'll have to try to get an extension on my loan application." Kim turned back to her careful breaking of eggs into the bowl. "How did it happen that you met him? Is the television segment shooting on the waterfront, too?"

"Not so far as I know. Anyhow, that's up to my brother. He heard that I was going to be up here in connection with *my* job, so he asked me to check out a few things for him."

"Like whether or not the Stratford still had four walls and whether we intended to keep our commitment for the time period he'd mentioned?"

"Something like that. Don't worry—I'll give him a good report. Incidentally, your cook will be back by then, won't he?" The last came when she poured the egg mixture into a frying pan which was obviously too hot.

"He promised that he would." The red in Kim's cheeks came mainly from annoyance rather than heat from the stove burner. Damn it all! She'd meant to have things perfect and had ignored the most basic principle of egg cookery. Even though she'd yanked the pan off as soon as she'd heard the sizzle, the omelet would be tough and too brown. Not only that, she'd forgotten the cheese.

"Shall I fix the toast?" Gray said, deciding he'd better do more than make conversation.

"If you don't mind. There's bread in that drawer below the toaster and butter somewhere—" She looked around, trying to remember where she'd put it.

"Right here." Gray rescued it from her elbow and wondered how he could offer to cook the next omelet. Better to have a burned offering than risk it, he decided, and took the saucer of butter over to the toaster. "How about coffee?"

Kim took a deep breath and then shoved the frying pan back on the burner so she could reach for a kettle. "I forgot about that. Would instant be all right?"

"It would certainly be faster," Gray said, with an eye on the omelet, which was once again frizzling around the edges.

At that moment the lights dipped and then came back to full power. Kim gave a silent prayer of thanks and then giggled as she realized what she'd done. Imagine being grateful for a power outage! Gray would think she'd gone completely berserk.

When she stole a glance under her lashes across the room, it was obvious that he thought exactly that. "I'm glad that you still have a sense of humor," he said finally, buttering the toast when it popped up. "Most people aren't ecstatic about a power failure."

"I've learned to give thanks for small favors," she told him, managing to slide the frying pan under the broiler to finish cooking the omelet without any further catastrophes. "Right now, if we get any kind of a dinner without having to resort to the fireplace, I'll consider it a minor miracle. Of course, there are always hot dogs and a toasting fork. No buns though."

Gray nodded grimly, not surprised by the last report. It fit in with the rest of the picture. He considered himself an enlightened male and realized that contemporary women no longer wanted to be chained to the kitchen stove. Logic failed him, though, when he saw Kim pull out the frying pan and survey the omelet, which had gotten even browner under the broiler. It was all very well for his landlady to look like a blond centerfold, but it wouldn't have hurt if she'd spent a little time studying a recipe book instead of her makeup.

"If your toast's ready, so is this," Kim said, trying

for a cheerful note as she slid the omelet onto a cold plate. "I'll bring the coffee when I finish cooking my omelet. It'll be more comfortable if you go in and eat in front of the fireplace."

Gray nodded and accepted his sparse dinner, wishing as he took a closer look that he could dispose of it in the blaze and go out for a hamburger.

Kim found him chewing valiantly through his main course when she came in a few minutes later, carrying a steaming cup of coffee, which she put on the small end table by the Victorian settee flanking the fireplace. "I forgot to ask if you wanted cream or sugar," she said, averting her glance from the plate he was balancing on his knees.

"No, thanks. Where's your dinner?"

"Just coming." She went over to peer through the drapes again, saying, "I don't like the sound of that wind. It might be a good idea to get the candles out." She moved over to the dining-room archway and disappeared around the corner, coming back an instant later with two cut-glass candelabra, which she put on the fireplace mantel. "There," she said with some satisfaction, "now we're ready for the worst!" And then as she saw him try to cut the leathery edge of his omelet, her shoulders shook with helpless laughter. "If it can get worse. That must be the most ghastly omelet in creation."

Her frank admission brought a reluctant grin to his face. "It'll never win any ribbons from Julia Child. If yours is anything like it, eat it while it's hot."

She pretended to consider. "Actually I thought it might be more appetizing in the dark." Her voice trailed off as the overhead lights dipped again, made a halfhearted attempt to come back to full power, and then disappeared completely. "Damn!" she said and reached for a box of matches on the shelf.

Gray took advantage of the firelit room to put his half-eaten omelet on the table at his side, retrieving his last piece of toast as he tried for a more comfortable position on the hard settee. "If I didn't know better," he said lazily, "I'd think you had second sight. Can you make the lights come back on when it's time to read in bed?"

Kim's smile held only a trace of humor as she lit the candelabra. "With the wind gusting like this, we'll be lucky to have power by morning, Mr. Stanton."

"Make that Gray instead of Mr. Stanton, will you? Or would these Victorian walls fall down at such heresy?"

Her smile deepened. "Considering the circumstances, I think it's all right."

"Good. Now take one of those candles and bring your dinner in here while I put another log on the fire."

When Kim reappeared she was carrying a small tray with cheese and crackers alongside her cup of coffee in one hand and a flashlight in the other. "I put the candelabrum down in your room," she confessed. "If you start freezing in the middle of the night, there are logs in the fireplace down there."

"I thought you were going to eat," Gray said, frowning.

"I am. Right now." She hesitated for a moment and then joined him on the curved settee, carefully depositing the cheese tray between them.

"What about your omelet?"

"I should give thanks that I had an excuse to dump

it in the garbage. It looked even worse than yours," she announced candidly. "I can recommend this Brie. Would you like some?"

Gray nodded and accepted a healthy wedge. He waited until she'd helped herself and then fell to.

"That makes up for any deficiencies in the first course," he told Kim after they'd demolished the plateful of cheese and crackers in a companionable silence.

"Unfortunately that's as much as I can offer," she said, finishing her last swallow of coffee. "Not that there's much entertainment here at any time. Usually we cater to guests who don't need it."

"The nearly-dead and newly-wed?"

"Mostly the latter," she said, with a grin. "They're not demanding at all."

"Umm." Gray yawned mightily and rested his head on the hardwood trim of the settee. "Right now I feel like that other classification. Lord knows why I'm so tired this early—except that it's been a full day. After I managed to get to the airport on time, I found my flight had been delayed."

"That's a natural hazard these days. Do you have to do a lot of traveling in your job?"

"More than I like. Fortunately the company is growing, so keeping busy is a healthy sign," he said, trying to smother another yawn.

"I don't imagine it helps your family life," Kim commented in a casual tone as she put the empty cheese platter on the table at her elbow.

Gray's eyebrows came together as he gave her a puzzled look. "What's that?"

Kim managed an innocent expression. "I just meant

that traveling complicates a marriage. It must be difficult for your wife and children."

"Since there's no wife and no children it hasn't bothered me," he said dryly. "The closest family tie I have now is my brother, Scott."

Gray's answer didn't give Kim any particular lift. Even if he didn't have a wife, it didn't mean that he was without feminine companionship. It was more likely that he had a beautiful girlfriend who would accept any role he chose—just to be a part of his life.

"What's wrong?"

His abrupt question cut through her woolgathering, and she glanced up to find him frowning again. "There's nothing wrong," she said hastily.

"You had a funny look on your face suddenly."

"No heat—no lights—and a fortune in groceries thawing in the freezer. Isn't that enough?"

"I guess so," he agreed ruefully. "This seems like a lot of responsibility for just one woman. Haven't you anybody to help? Like a husband or children?" The last was tacked on quite deliberately—showing that he was well aware she'd been fishing before.

She shook her head. "No husband—no children."

"No boyfriend lurking in the bushes?"

Kim's eyebrows went up at that query, and he went on to explain. "I just meant that you could use some muscles and extra bodies around here. Of course, I'll be glad to do what I can—"

"That won't be necessary," she cut in, getting to her feet.

He stood up beside her, taking his time about it as he directed an assessing glance at the fireplace. "I don't know about that. We could use more wood for that fireplace if the heat's going to be off for long, and you'd better be making arrangements for ice to save the stuff in the freezer."

"I'll face that problem tomorrow . . ."

"What about family?" he interrupted, sticking to his line of thought with disconcerting ease. "Didn't you say you'd been brought up in Port Lathrop?"

"I'm fresh out of relatives at the moment," she said, her chin going up defiantly. "My parents usually spend the summer here, but right now they're somewhere in the Indian Ocean on a freighter trip. Besides, I don't need to go running for help. If you can manage in your room tonight, I should have things under control in the morning. And if you go down now, there might still be some hot water left in the heater if you want a shower or bath."

Gray's lips twitched at her "Here's your hat, what's your hurry" attitude, although he could sympathize with her dilemma. Even with all systems working, it didn't take any imagination to see that the Stratford could be a handful. And despite Kim's outward determination not to panic, he knew that she was well aware of the disasters a prolonged storm could cause. It showed in the rigidity of her shoulders as she put the firescreen in place and the way her fingers trembled when she handed him the flashlight.

"This should help you on the stairs down to your room," she said.

"What about you?" he asked, watching her carefully.

"I have another one in the kitchen."

"Okay, then." He lingered a minute longer, oddly reluctant to leave her in the big, high-ceilinged room, which felt damp and chilled as soon as he moved away from the fire. The drafts were strong enough to move the fringe on that monstrous beaded lampshade near the window, he thought, and added aloud, "You're sure there's nothing I can do to help?"

"Quite sure, thanks." Kim was proud of the brisk assurance in her tone.

"And you will go to bed?" When her eyes widened, he went on hurriedly, "No sitting up to check on wind damage or trying to stay awake?"

She shook her head again. "No, I promise. Besides, I probably wouldn't hear it if the roof blew off. My mother and father never let me forget that I slept soundly through an earthquake once."

"The sign of a clear conscience," Gray said lightly. "Okay, I'll be on my way. If the roof blows off, I won't even mention it until breakfast time. Goodnight."

"Goodnight," Kim said. "I hope tomorrow will be better for you."

He gave her a quizzical smile and headed through the archway toward the back of the inn and the stair to the basement.

Although it was far too expensively decorated to be called just a basement anymore, Kim thought, as she watched the dim glow of his flashlight disappear. Her expression became bleak when she surveyed the big cold empty rooms around her. Until that moment, she hadn't been aware how much comfort Gray Stanton's presence had provided. By rights, she should have been paying *him* for spending the night. Certainly she wouldn't charge him for the fiasco. She shuddered when she thought of the omelet he'd consumed and wondered why the fates had to interfere between a man and a woman just when something promising might have developed. Nothing at all permanent, she told herself hastily, but at least under ordinary conditions he wouldn't have looked back on his night in Port Lathrop with loathing.

The sound of something metallic hitting the ground outside brought her out of her reverie, and she hurried to pull aside the window drape, peering out into the darkness. It was impossible to see anything on the side lawn and certainly raining too hard for her to investigate. Probably it had been a piece of flashing from the front chimney, she concluded, after going over some grim possibilities. That could mean another leak in the roof or a blocked gutter, if any other parts had fallen.

If the latter happened, the basement could be ankle-deep by morning. Kim hesitated as she thought about going down to warn Gray and then shook her head. There would be time enough later if the worst *did* happen. It would be best if she spent the night in the room adjoining his to make sure that everything was all right. By daylight, she'd simply move back to her bedroom upstairs. It was a practical solution as well, because the second floor without heat rivaled the plains of Siberia, and it wasn't worthwhile starting another fireplace fire in her regular bedroom.

She took the remaining candles and did a cursory check of the windows on the main floor to make sure there wasn't any drastic leaking going on. After that was finished to her satisfaction, she took the cheese tray back out to the kitchen and tidied things there. Finally she went up the creaking stairs to her room on the second floor and changed hurriedly into pajamas and a tartan wool robe. The bedroom temperature wasn't like Siberia, she told herself as she tied the belt on her robe, it was strictly from the Antarctic.

When she descended to the lower level five minutes later, she was happy to find that it was considerably warmer there. Not only that, the floor in the hallway was blessedly dry and there was only a slight dampness at the bottom of the outside door. So far, so good, she thought happily and moved quietly back to the room she'd chosen.

She lingered for just an instant outside Gray's bedroom door, noting a silence on the other side. He must have decided that an early night was the simplest solution. Even so, she took care opening her door so that he wouldn't be disturbed and, just as quietly, turned back the covers on her bed to slip into it. She shivered in the icy sheets for a few minutes, but soon the warmth from the down comforter penetrated and she was able to stretch out and relax. The room was an exact twin to the one she'd allotted to Gray, and she wondered why she hadn't chosen it for her stay in the first place. Certainly the furnishings were nicer, and if the stormy weather continued, the view from her upstairs window would merely be fog and rain. Perhaps tomorrow she'd move down permanently, she thought, stretching even more luxuriously and finding a soft spot on the pillow. In her mind, she checked off all the things she still had to do at the crack of dawn and murmured with satisfaction that she'd remembered to put matches next to the candles. She hadn't brought an alarm clock, but she certainly could set her mental one, and it hadn't failed her before. On that comforting thought, she yawned again and was sound asleep ten seconds later.

Chapter Three

When the irritating noise finally penetrated Gray's consciousness in the middle of the night, he did his level best to ignore it. Even half asleep he knew that all the heat in his bedroom had disappeared, and with the storm raging outside, the electricity was still out. At that moment, another series of penetrating sounds came from the hallway, and he pushed up on an elbow, trying to identify the noise. If he didn't know better, he could swear that a chicken was squawking nearby, except that chickens didn't squawk at—he squinted at his watch, trying to read the luminous dial, and then swore softly—even in Port Lathrop no chicken would be fool enough to sound off at four-thirty on a dark morning.

The noises came stridently again, and with them came recognition. It was a battery-operated smoke alarm, and from the sound of things, the battery was on its last legs. Unless somebody did something, the alarm would continue to wind down with its noisy blasts for another hour.

When the sound erupted five minutes later, Gray shoved the covers back with a fervent "Dammit to hell!" and groped for the flashlight on the bedside table.

He switched it on and managed to find his slippers, but it took a little longer to unearth his travel robe from the suitcase. If he'd known how cold it was going to be, he'd have brought a wool one rather than the dark-blue silk one he slipped on. It was a token gesture at best, he told himself. Obviously he wasn't about to encounter his landlady on the way—that smoke alarm must have been burping at intervals for some time, and, from the quiet in the basement hallway, he was the only one who was aware of it. It wasn't surprising, he told himself as he directed the dim beam of the flashlight down the corridor. Probably Kim Cosgrove had installed herself in one of the suites on the second or third floor where she was safe from minor disturbances.

The alarm sounded again—apparently from a closed door just ahead of him. Gray gave a silent prayer that the room wasn't locked and sighed with relief when the heavy door opened under his touch.

The feeble beam of his flashlight showed that it was a combination linen and storage room and only took a minute more to find the smoke alarm located next to a ceiling beam. Sure enough, the red flag was down on the side, showing that the battery needed replacing. Another strident beep erupting from it even as he approached made Gray wince. No wonder he couldn't sleep through it!

He glanced around the open shelves of a storage cabinet nearby, although he didn't really expect to find a replacement battery. Miss Cosgrove was doing her best to look like the efficient landlady, but at the moment, the odds were against her. Well, the Stratford Inn would just have to do without a smoke alarm on the lower level for the rest of the night. He found a wooden box to serve as a stool and then struggled, one-handed, to remove the alarm cover. It stuck stubbornly on one corner, despite his efforts. Gray swore under his breath and rested the flashlight on the edge of the shelf at his elbow. That left the alarm barely visible, but he was able to use two hands and wrench the cover off. He stood clutching it in one hand while he squinted up to find the wires to disengage at the battery terminals. Then, with another exasperated sigh, he put the alarm cover on a convenient shelf and took up the flashlight to make sure that he pulled the proper connection. The alarm started to sound off again, but the noise stopped abruptly as Gray yanked on the wires.

He gave a grunt of satisfaction and stepped back, forgetting that he was so near to the edge of the box. Suddenly finding himself with one foot in midair, he naturally grabbed at the edge of the shelf to regain his balance. He forgot that he was clutching the flashlight at the time, and it promptly fell on the linoleum floor. Gray uttered a pithy comment about the status of the world in general as he retrieved the flashlight and gave it an impatient shake, trying to restore the flickering beam to full power.

The therapy didn't work; in keeping with the rest of the happenings at the Stratford, it went from bad to worse. An instant later, Gray found himself standing completely in the dark with a useless flashlight in his hand.

There was more conversation under his breath which didn't bear repeating as he searched the pockets of his robe for a pack of matches and instead found only a clean handkerchief.

That left a trip back to his room in the complete

darkness. Fortunately, once he got into the hall there was no danger of tripping over obstacles, he told himself, trying to find something cheerful about wandering around a strange basement at four-thirty in the morning. Plus the fact that the damned smoke alarm wouldn't be sounding off every thirty seconds.

He left the useless flashlight on a counter en route to the hall door and carefully maneuvered back the way he'd come. As he moved along the wall, he tried to remember which door was his and then decided that there definitely hadn't been an intervening one before he'd reached the storage room.

He smiled with satisfaction when his exploring fingers finally encountered the familiar door jamb. Opening it, he thought for a moment about lighting the candles on his bed table and then decided against it. There wasn't much more time before dawn, and he felt as if he could sleep for a month! Probably it would take that long before he managed to get warm again.

He reached the mattress after stubbing his slipper on the leg of the piecrust bed table and finally shrugged out of his robe. After tossing it toward the foot of the bed, he reached automatically for the pillow with his other hand.

Ten seconds later he was stretched out comfortably under the down comforter, and two seconds after that he was sound asleep.

When the disturbance came in the hallway, it was considerably later. Enough so that pale daylight seeped around the edge of the velvet drapes. Kim groaned slightly and buried her nose in her pillow, reluctant to start another day. From the sound of masculine voices in the hallway, the carpenter had arrived for his morning shift, and evidently he'd brought a helper with him. That meant she'd better get cracking, because it wouldn't be much longer until her only guest would be wanting breakfast. Her eyes came wide open at that, and she snaked an arm from under the covers to check and see if the light worked on her bed table. The resultant glow brought a smile to her face, which changed to stark horror as a male voice behind her said thickly, "For God's sake—turn off the light. I'd like to get *some* sleep . . ."

She never did hear the end of his sentence, because at that moment the hall door opened and she found herself staring at two men who stared back, goggle-eyed, from the threshold. Kim rallied quickly enough to identify the muscular figure of Ozzie Halvorson, Port Lathrop's middle-aged carpenter. Beside him stood John Amherst, immaculate as always in a dark business suit.

Kim made a belated grab at the sheet as she saw Amherst's expression change to a frown as his gaze lingered on her wrinkled pajama top before moving on. "I didn't know you were coming," she began, trying to sound dignified and then spoiled the effect with a "Good God!" when the male figure beside her in bed surged upward, taking her sheet with him in the process.

"What in the devil is this?" he complained bitterly, squinting at the two men in the doorway. "I don't remember issuing any invitations . . ." His own voice trailed off as his gaze focused on Kim's still body beside him in bed. "Bloody hell!" he muttered, suddenly figuring out what had happened.

"I'm terribly sorry, Kim," John Amherst broke into the thick silence. "When Ozzie told me I might find you down here I had no idea I'd be invading your—privacy."

"I'll be goin' back to work," the Norwegian said, his neck red as he tried to avoid looking in the room. "That storm raised Cain with the bay window, so I'll need more lumber," he began and then realized that his employer was scarcely in a position to discuss it. "I see you later."

He had scarcely gone out the door when Amherst turned to follow him, disapproval showing in every inch of his being.

"This is not what you think, Amherst," Gray said, annoyed to be convicted without a hearing. "Kim and I were up most of the night because of the storm, so we have an excuse for sleeping in."

The older man turned on the threshold, a frown marring his usually jovial countenance. "When I saw you yesterday, you didn't mention that you knew Kim."

Gray felt the girl beside him stiffen, but he spoke up before she could interrupt. "I guess it's impossible to keep anything a secret in a small town. We should have known better," he said ruefully.

As Gray's words sank in, the businessman's expression went from disapproval to doubt and then to incredulity. He turned back to Kim, saying, "I had no idea. When did all this happen? Have you even told your parents about this?"

"Well—no." Kim suddenly became aware of what he was thinking and tried feverishly to find a respectable explanation for being discovered in bed with a stranger. "Mother and Dad are in the middle of the Indian Ocean right now, so it's a little hard to get in touch."

"Then you must let me stand in for them. There's no reason you can't have a reception at my house. Of course, I can't promise that Gerald will do any celebrating. You haven't told him, have you?"

"She didn't have a chance. I wasn't sure that I could get away to join her until the last minute," Gray interrupted.

"That's all right." Amherst beamed on them as he stepped out into the hallway and reached for the doorknob. "This way you can combine business and a honeymoon. All the better. I'll go up and make some coffee now—you look as if you could use it."

As the door closed firmly behind him, Kim whirled to face Gray's still figure. "Did you hear what he said?"

"Honeymoon," Gray repeated woodenly, leaning back against the head of the bed. "My Lord, I didn't know he was going to take it that way."

"He wouldn't have if you'd just let me explain," Kim countered furiously.

"Don't be a fool!" Gray made no effort to hide his disdain. "You could have talked until you were blue in the face and it wouldn't have made any difference. Besides, what could you tell him?"

"What you were doing here, for one thing." She paused, frowning fiercely. "What in the hell *are* you doing in my bed?"

"I didn't know I *was* in it." Seeing her seething expression, he went on even more forcefully. "It's the truth. I must have come in the wrong door after I disconnected the smoke alarm."

"You did what?"

"Just what I said. I don't know how you managed to sleep through its exploding every thirty seconds," he accused. "I can tell you one thing, if I'd known you were sleeping down here, I would have pounded on the wall instead of doing a Boy Scout act."

Kim pulled the sheet up to her chin again with a decisive movement. "All you had to do was check the number on the door."

"I would have been glad to," he replied in a dangerously level tone, "except that I dropped that miserable flashlight you gave me when I was trying to fix the alarm. Unless I wanted to spend the rest of the night in that room, I had to come back by Braille. I found this door and felt my way to the bed. Unfortunately," he added with a bitter tinge, "it's a big bed and you must have been on the other side at the time. I sure as hell didn't mean to get—" He stopped angrily in midsentence, aware he was on dangerous ground.

"You've made your point. And that explanation is so cockeyed that it's probably true." She sighed and bit her lip. "Unfortunately, here at Port Lathrop, not only the houses are Victorian. It's the state of mind."

He nodded, obviously trying to subdue his temper. "I didn't mean to sound as if I don't approve of marriage."

"That's big of you," she announced, cutting him off again. Pushing the covers back, she swung her legs out of bed. "Never mind, I'll set everybody straight as soon as I get upstairs."

"The devil you will!" He gave the sheet a look of disdain as he shoved it away and got out on his side. Cinching up the belt on his pajamas, he came around the footboard and started toward the door. "I got you into this mess—I'll get you out of it. One way or another."

Kim grabbed his arm when he tried to pass by, so upset by his announcement that she forgot her pajamas were an old pair which had shrunk in repeated washings. "What's that supposed to mean?" she asked, standing firm.

"Just what I said." In the process of lifting her restraining hand, his masculine glance raked over her curved figure and then came slowly back to her face. "Who's Gerald?" he asked abruptly.

"I beg your pardon."

"You heard me." The impatience came back to his voice. "Although if you could sleep through that smoke alarm, maybe you *should* get your hearing checked."

"There's nothing wrong with my ears. It's your mind that gallops all over the countryside." Then with another quick look at his unyielding expression, she said, "Gerald Amherst—he's John's son. A sort of—friend of mine. I've known him for years off and on."

"Damnation! This is more complicated than I imagined. Never mind, if he's worth having—he'll believe what you say."

"It really doesn't matter." Kim tried to sound as if she believed it. "Anyhow, the sooner I get dressed, the sooner it will all be over."

"You're probably right." Gray gave her outgrown pajamas another look and then reached for her robe, which had slithered halfway off the bed. "I think you'd better put this on before you streak through the kitchen en route to your clothes—wherever they are."

Kim looked down at herself and gasped, sliding

quickly into the robe he was holding. "They're upstairs. I'd forgotten I'd changed rooms."

"So I gathered." He jerked his head toward the half-open armoire against the wall, which showed an empty interior. "You never explained what *you* were doing down here. Is mattress testing part of your landlady role, or do you play musical beds from choice?"

"Of course not." His dispassionate expression made her add, "I was worried about seepage."

"Seepage? I thought that only happened in cemeteries. Especially Louisiana ones."

"I'm talking about moisture coming in the door," she said, giving an impatient tug to the belt of her robe. "I didn't think you'd be thrilled to wake up in a waterbed when you hadn't started out in one."

He rubbed his neck as if the conversation were taking a heavy toll so early in the morning. "This place has more hazards than a public golf course. Now what's bothering you?" The last came as he saw her preoccupied expression.

"I was just thinking that maybe it would be better if we presented a united front when I meet John upstairs. Will it take you long to shave and get some clothes on?"

"Probably not." He moved toward the door again. "Is there any hot water, or would that be expecting too much?"

"I honestly don't know."

Seeing her embarrassment, he sighed and said, "Hell! I'm sorry. There's no excuse for taking out my bad temper on you. Besides, it won't be the first time I've shaved in cold water. Are you going to wait here?"

She shook her head. "There's a back staircase. With any luck, I can get up to my bedroom without running into any more bank directors. Maybe you could come on up when you're ready and we can compare ideas."

"Or explanations?"

" 'Alibi' might be closer to the truth," she said ruefully.

"You don't have to look so guilty," he reminded her. "After all, nothing happened."

"I know that and you know that, but . . ."

He put up a hand in defense. "Okay, I get the idea. Give me fifteen minutes. Even less if there isn't any hot water." Opening the door to his bedroom, he paused on the threshold. "How do I find you upstairs? I can't go around knocking on doors. Besides, it's a little late for that."

"You said it—I didn't," she retorted and then put her hands up to press either side of her temples. "Sorry, I didn't mean to sound like a fishwife. My bedroom's the one overlooking the Strait—I'll leave the door ajar."

Kim stood where she was after he disappeared into his room, vitally aware of the circumstances stacked against them. It was about as easy to change John Amherst's mind as to derail one of those long freight trains delivering cargo to his wharves, and she knew only too well that his son's reaction was going to be decidedly caustic when he heard. Even old Ozzie wouldn't be above passing a choice bit of gossip when the rare occasion arose. Kim spared time for a last despairing look back at the big double bed and then went down the hall toward the rear stairs.

Her old room on the second floor was a restful

haven when she slipped into it a minute later and closed the door firmly behind her. She'd heard John Amherst's voice as she'd passed the kitchen door, but a quick peek through the glass aperture showed that he was on the telephone with his back to her, so she hadn't lingered. The sound of hammering nearby was evidence that old Ozzie was working at the end of the hall—in the latest conversion of a mammoth closet to a modern bathroom. The thought of how much that was going to cost brought another frown to Kim's face and she was tempted to crawl under the down comforter on the big cherrywood four-poster and not come out for six months.

That ludicrous fantasy made her smile and shake her head as she went into her adjoining bathroom. It wasn't nearly as luxurious as some of Ozzie's recent conversions, but at least it was paid for and—she turned the porcelain faucet at the tub—for once the water was hot.

She didn't waste any time after that; the way her luck was running Gray would arrive before she got dressed and give her another of those level looks which made her feel two inches tall. In her hurry to rinse off the soap, she turned the cold-water tap more forcefully than she'd planned and gasped at the shock. At least it accomplished one objective, she told herself as she hurriedly stepped out onto the mat and reached for a bath sheet—it effectively cleared any fuzzy-headed thoughts. There was only one sensible thing to do, and that was simply go down and tell John Amherst the truth.

The sooner the better, she decided, hanging the towel on a rack and reaching for her clean underthings. She chose a slip instead of a camisole top, deciding that a dress might add a little dignity to the occasion rather than her usual outfit of jeans or tired corduroys. She sorted quickly through the hangers in her closet and finally chose a cotton print in soft shades of brown with a blouson top and dolman sleeves, which she pushed up impatiently once she dragged it over her head. There was a long zipper at the back of the neckline, and she reached for it automatically—groaning "Oh, no!" when it snagged halfway up.

"I thought you were going to leave the door open," Gray accused her from the threshold. "I've been going around like a peeping Tom up here, expecting to get caught any minute. What in the devil are you doing?" The last came as she tried a contortionist maneuver that defied description, yanking on the stuck zipper.

"What does it look like?" she flared. "This miserable thing's stuck and I can't get it to move."

"What miserable thing?"

She straightened and said forcefully, "My zipper, of course. What do you think I'm talking about?"

"I haven't been sure most of the time. No, don't run off in a huff. I can fix a zipper, for God's sake. Come over here by the window so I can see properly." He took a moment to stroke aside a strand of her pale, silky hair, which nestled at her collar.

"Can't you fix it?"

Kim's anxious question brought him back to earth, and he bent over her again. "I see what's wrong. One of the zipper teeth is caught on the material underneath. Damn! It's really wedged. I may have to tear it a little."

"Must you?" She glanced awkwardly over her shoulder at his intent profile. "If I could only get the dress over my head, I probably could fix it without that."

"Well, it'll be a tight squeeze, but we can give it a try. I'll pull your skirt up and get that out of the way—oh, hell!"

"What's the matter?" Kim asked, her voice muffled when the voluminous material of her skirt shrouded her head under Gray's helping hand.

"Things are hung up on a ribbon," he muttered. "Darned if I know where it came from." There was a momentary pause and then he said accusingly, "It's attached to your slip."

Belatedly Kim remembered the white satin ribbon which threaded through her bodice and decorated the flounce at her hemline. "Don't tell me that's caught in the zipper, too."

"No, dammit. It's caught on my watch strap. Half a minute—I'm almost free."

Suddenly the ridiculousness of the situation got the better of Kim and she sagged against him, giggling helplessly. "This is *too* much," she began and then laughed harder than ever as her wide skirt draped over Gray's head and shoulders while he yanked at the thin satin ribbon caught on his gold watch.

"I'm sorry to break up the party."

There wasn't any humor whatsoever on the face of the man who spoke from the doorway. "Dad said you'd just gotten up, so I didn't think you were planning to go *back* to bed."

Kim shot him a stricken look and clutched Gray's shoulder, trying to pull her skirt down. "Gerald! How did you get here so quickly? For heaven's sake— don't get the wrong idea!" Even as she defended herself, she saw that Gray had to tear the piece of satin ribbon from his watch strap before he could separate himself from the flounce on her slip. When he straightened to turn and face the other man, she said tightly, "Gray, this is John's son—Gerald Amherst." Her chin went up as she turned toward the door again. "Gerald—Gray Stanton."

"So I've heard." The newcomer made no effort to advance into the bedroom and shake hands. Instead, he stood stiffly on the threshold and surveyed them with disdain.

Kim was thinking that it wasn't a pose which came easily to him. For one thing, his round face made him look younger than his thirty years, and his wide mouth was normally curved in laughter rather than the grim, level line of it then. He'd obviously dressed in a hurry, because his sport shirt was jammed into the belt of his cotton slacks and his thick fair hair was standing on end, as if he hadn't bothered to comb it. Her suspicion was confirmed when he said accusingly, "Dad just called to give me the news. I think you might have told me, Kim. Or were you going to mention it tonight on our dinner date?"

She winced under his sarcasm, but Gray spoke up before she could reply. "Actually, Kim didn't know that I was going to be able to make it for the weekend."

Gerald let his angry gaze rest on the other man. "I don't see what that has to do with Kim's telling me she was married. My God"—he turned back to her in sudden rage—"I'd planned to propose to you tonight."

"Gerald, I'm sorry—if you'll just let me explain . . ." Kim was stopped by Gray's painful warning pressure on her wrist.

"You can blame me for all the secrecy," he told Gerald in a businesslike way. "There were family reasons. I'm sorry that you got caught in the middle.

I know that . . ." He paused for a split second, then went on as if there hadn't been a break. "I know that my wife didn't lead you on under false pretenses."

Kim gasped at his audacity and said, "This is really absurd—"

"You don't have to explain Kim to me," Gerald cut in angrily, ignoring her as he stared defiantly at Gray. "I've known her all my life, for God's sake. That's why I thought Dad and I deserved better treatment." His expression crumpled suddenly, and he shook his head as if to clear it. "I can't believe it, even now."

Kim shook off Gray's grip and started toward him. "Gerald, this has gotten completely out of hand. I don't even know where to start—" She was brought up short when Gray moved swiftly and caught her to him, his lean fingers tightening on her shoulder so that she gave a surprised whimper.

"We can do the explanations at breakfast if it's really necessary," he said, his glance daring her to contradict him. "Right now, I could do with some coffee. I think your father mentioned something about getting it ready," he told Gerald.

"I suppose so." The stocky young man took an unwilling step back into the hallway. "If he had time between phone calls. I know that he was sending a radiogram to your folks when I arrived," he told Kim. "It took me a while to find you up here." From Gerald's grim tone, he was obviously remembering the scene he'd interrupted, fantasizing that it would have been even more embarrassing if he'd come a little later.

Kim stared at him, glassy-eyed, her own thoughts in an entirely different channel. "A radiogram to

Mother and Dad?" she repeated incredulously. "For heaven's sake, why?"

"To congratulate them, of course. It's the decent thing to do. And he was letting them know he'd organize a celebration and reception, since they weren't here to hold it."

"How—how thoughtful of him," Kim managed finally and sent an imploring glance in Gray's direction, hoping there was something he could say or do to pull them out of the morass.

At that moment, the shrilling noise of a doorbell pealed through the house. It was a demanding ring, followed promptly by another. Whoever was on the front porch wasn't taking any chances of being ignored.

"Ozzie must have finally fixed that bell," Kim said after the second ring. "I'd better go answer it. Unless you think your father will." She looked at Gerald, who immediately shook his head.

"I imagine he's still on the phone," he told them and then gave an exasperated sigh as the sharp bell cut through the air again. "Never mind, I'll go. I might as well." His annoyed gaze lingered on the other two. "There isn't anything I can do here."

The last sentence was tossed over his shoulder as he turned back into the hall.

He was barely out of earshot when Kim wheeled on Gray. "My God! This is like a nightmare," she gasped. "If it keeps up, there's no explanation that they'll believe."

Gray shoved his hands in the pockets of his trousers and glared back at her. "You're telling me! I thought your friend Gerald was going for my throat. Why didn't you say that you had a disappointed lover in the wings?"

Kim's chin came up. "He's *not* my lover. I've been trying to discourage him since he was eighteen years old. That isn't important. All I want now is to go downstairs and make sure that his father gets off the phone before he calls in our happy tidings to the White House." She tried to pull the neckline of her dress around so that she could reach the stuck zipper. "But first I have to get out of this thing. You didn't help at all," she accused Gray as an afterthought. "It's still stuck."

"I know that. And I don't think you can get it off over your head," he added, carefully keeping his hands in his pockets as he scrutinized the offending zipper again.

"Then I'll just have to rip the thing. I refuse to spend the rest of the month like this."

"Nobody's asking you to."

"Well, go ahead," she prodded impatiently when he didn't make a move. "Rip it. As carefully as you can. That way I can fix it later—somehow."

"Okay. I don't suppose it matters now." Gray glanced over his shoulder before he reached for her again. "We've already been tagged with adultery in the basement and indecent exposure a few minutes ago. There's not much left."

Kim nodded, trying to watch what he was doing over her shoulder. "At least there's nobody else to come and interrupt at this point. Yank it," she instructed impatiently when he didn't make any progress. "That binding tape is tough."

"Okay, here goes."

The material gave way when the stuck teeth of the zipper suddenly parted. Kim staggered slightly and felt an unexpected draft on her back as her bodice fell forward. That, however, was nothing compared to the chill that came over her as a feminine voice shrilled, "Gray, whatever are you doing?" And Gerald's incredulous comment, "My God! He's at it again."

As Kim whirled around, she caught a glance of Gray shaking his head in resignation. "I don't understand," she began, only to have him say reluctantly,

"I'm not surprised. Carola, what in the devil are you doing here?"

"I was a bridesmaid at a friend's wedding in Vancouver yesterday," the young woman in the doorway replied. "When I called Scott afterward, he mentioned that you were practically in the neighborhood. But this man"—she fluttered an anxious hand toward Gerald beside her—"told me you were up here with your wife. I was sure it was a mistake."

"It's certainly a mistake as far as I'm concerned," Gerald put in with a sour expression.

Kim was trying to pull her dress back to a measure of respectability, but she had time to note the striking beauty of the other woman. Her classic features and long brown hair, which was pulled back with a ribbon at her nape, made her age hard to assess. Probably in her early twenties, Kim guessed. There certainly wasn't anything juvenile about her figure in the nubbly red bouclé knit suit which clung like a second skin. If her petulant expression was anything to go by, the lady had money, and a possessive claim on Gray, and was madder than hell at what she'd found in the bedroom. At least she could do something about that, Kim decided, and said, "I'm sorry about all this—er—Carola. Gray and I can explain—"

"Later," Gray cut in, putting a protective arm around her shoulders. "In the meantime, Kim, this is Carola Kenyon, my brother's intended."

The brown-haired girl stared at them, a succession of emotions going over her perfect features. "You mean it's true?"

Kim felt Gray's clasp tighten as he said, "Well, I'd hardly be playing games in a place like Port Lathrop."

"But you never mentioned getting married," Carola went on defiantly when Gray merely lifted his eyebrows. "This isn't like you."

"So Dad and I weren't the only ones kept in the dark," Gerald interposed, his voice getting back to normal. "It must have been the best-kept secret on the coast. Although, frankly, I can't see why all the hush-hush tactics unless . . ."

The way his glance went to Kim's waist showed the direction his suspicions were taking, and Gray cut in angrily, "Maybe we wanted a little privacy before our friends got together and turned it into a three-ring circus."

Carola swallowed and looked paler than before at his accusation but rallied quickly. "You must admit that this is a queer spot to hear the news. I didn't think you'd pick a place like this for a honeymoon."

"He didn't have much choice," Kim felt compelled to say. "I own the Stratford."

The other young woman's face registered the shock of that while Gerald was saying stoutly, "I don't see anything wrong with the inn—it's one of the finest examples of Victorian architecture on the Pacific Coast."

"Well, I didn't mean anything slanderous—" Carola began.

"I know that," Gray cut in, not letting her compound the felony, "but you'd better stop while you're ahead. Otherwise Kim will think you're sadly lacking in manners. Just go on down and see if there's coffee, would you? We could all use some."

"You'll be down, too, won't you?" Carola asked him. "You're not going to stay up here." Her mutinous glance went around the bedroom as if she still couldn't believe her eyes.

"We'll both be down," Gray told her. "Just as soon as Kim can change."

"Sometimes he lets me get in a word or two. On good days, even a whole sentence," Kim told them, irritated to find that Gray was taking over again.

"I'm sorry, darling." Despite his words, Gray's tone was unrepentant and there was a warning in the sharp glance he bestowed on her. "If you don't need my help, I'll go along with Carola and Gerald." He turned to usher the other two out into the hallway and saw them started down the curving stairway. Before following, he snapped his fingers in exasperation. "Damn! I forgot to tell Kim something. Save me a cup of coffee," he ordered Carola when she would have lingered, as well.

Without wasting any more time, he moved swiftly back into the bedroom and closed the door firmly behind him. He caught Kim in the process of stepping out of her dress, and she looked up, startled.

"Good Lord! *Now* what?" she asked.

"You can go on with that," he said. "I just wanted to check with you that we have a straight story on this. It won't do to have you telling Gerald that we tied the knot last week while I'm convincing Carola that it was a month and a half ago in Nevada."

Kim stared at him, her lips parted in amazement. "You mean you're going through with this? You can't be serious!"

"The hell I'm not. Through no fault of ours, both families are involved at this point," he told her grimly. "God knows what your parents will think after getting that radiogram. Then there's my brother. Maybe I could explain to Scott, but Carola . . ." He shook his head. "It would be easier to get married and have the thing annulled in a few weeks. If that's acceptable to you."

The last was tacked on as an afterthought, Kim noticed, and she sank onto the edge of the bed, still in her slip. She folded her torn dress almost absently as she mulled over Gray's decision.

"Well, what do you say?" he asked as the silence lengthened.

"I guess you're right."

Her words emerged slowly and sounded unreal as they came to her ears. Gray wasn't unaware of her pale cheeks and taut expression, but he tried to keep sympathy from his tone. At that point, he told himself, there was no time to waste on frills or excuses. "Okay, I'll go down and face the inquisition. Thank God I haven't unpacked much. I should imagine that an overnight bag is all you'll need."

Kim's eyes widened as she stared across the room at him by the door. "Now what are you talking about?"

"We'll have to make it legal," he said in a low tone that wasn't any the less definite because of it. "And we sure as hell can't trot down here to the local city hall. For the record, we're starting out for a belated weekend honeymoon. Actually . . ." He swallowed as if stricken by the enormity of what he was about to say.

Kim took up where he left off. "We have to get married. Is that it?"

His stern mouth softened into a wry, crooked grin. "At the risk of sounding like somebody holding a shotgun, my dear Kimberly, that's precisely it."

Chapter Four

"Why is it that I feel as if we're being run out of town on a rail?" Kimberly asked Gray an hour or so later when they finally pulled away from the curb of the inn in his car. "I know it was too much to expect them to throw rice or orange blossoms, but you'd think we'd committed some terrible sin from the looks on their faces. Carola was practically crying." She glanced through the rear-window corner to see again the stocky figures of John Amherst and Gerald flanking Carola Kenyon's petite one on the inn's porch, gazing somberly after them.

"I know. Considering Gerald's farewell, I'm surprised that he didn't slash my tires as a final gesture," Gray said, slowing to turn a corner and then accelerating down the hill toward the highway.

"He wasn't exactly charming," Kim acknowledged, strangely relieved to be on their way. "Even so, his attitude made more sense than Carola's. If she's engaged to your brother, why does she have such a proprietary attitude toward you?"

Gray shrugged, keeping his glance straight ahead. "She's young—"

"Not that young."

"Well, maybe it's because I knew her first." He

braked for a stop sign and turned onto the busy highway leading out of town. "I was the one who introduced her to Scott. Carola's the type of woman who never crosses anybody out of her little black book." The last sentence was said with some bitterness, and Kim shot him a suspicious sideways glance.

"Maybe she wasn't playing by the same rules as you were."

"It wasn't the kind of relationship that needed any rules. She's a nice girl, but not my type." Gray took his attention from the traffic long enough to direct a quelling look at Kim's intent figure. "However, if she's going to be my sister-in-law, I can't very well push her onto the next plane south without any explanations—as much as I'd have liked to."

From the stern set of his jaw, Kim felt that he was contemplating a far more drastic fate for the lovely Carola just then. It wasn't the tone or sentiment of a man who was driving away from his true love, she decided. Although from the last look she'd had of Carola's woebegone face, she doubted if all her affection had been transferred to Gray's brother.

"I'm sorry that things turned into such a dreadful mess," Kim said, when the silence had lengthened between them.

Gray merely nodded and seemed to be concentrating on how to find a safe place to pass the camper truck which was being driven at a leisurely speed down the curving highway ahead of them.

When he made no attempt to say anything once they'd passed the offender, Kim went on determinedly, "At least you might tell me where we're going. That is, if you know."

"It isn't a habit of mine to drive around just for the

hell of it," he informed her in a disparaging tone. "I thought we'd do best someplace where we wouldn't stand out in the crowd. It has to be close enough so that we can get the license today. That way, we can just take the weekend off and still satisfy the three-day waiting period. I have to be back to work on Monday afternoon," he added, his brows drawing together as he thought about it. "That's why I picked Port Victor."

Kim nodded slowly. The town was one of the fastest-growing ones in the state and was a hub of tourist activity located on the busy Strait across from Vancouver Island. "At least we'll be safe for a week," she said. "Until the local paper comes out with vital statistics."

"Don't worry about that. I'll have a word with the clerks in the license bureau. With a good enough story, we can stay off the list."

"They'll probably think the worst, too."

Gray took his attention from driving long enough to send a sardonic glance her way. "At this point, we're used to it." His gaze lingered on her white turtleneck sweater worn with a mulberry jacket and pants. "I hope you brought something else to wear. If you go to the license bureau in that rig, they'll be bound to think the worst."

"Why? There's nothing wrong with wool slacks and a jacket." Her chin went up defiantly. "I *did* bring a couple of dresses, but I was saving them. And if my appearance embarrasses you, I can stay in the car while you register at the motel."

"There's nothing wrong with that getup," he said through a tightly held jaw, "it's just that you look about sixteen in it."

"That's ridiculous." Kim's tone was softer, but she was still visibly annoyed. "After everything that's happened today, I feel about fifty, or even older if you want the truth."

"Well, you don't look it. At least I can't be accused of hauling a minor across state lines. That's about the only crime left."

"I know." Kim sank dispiritedly into the corner of the seat and toyed with the plush edging of her jacket. "My mother and father are going to be sending cables like mad when they hear from Mr. Amherst. Did you ever get in touch with your brother?"

"No, thank the Lord. Carola was doing her best to reach him on the phone, but she didn't make it."

"It didn't do much for Gerald's disposition when you wouldn't say where we were going." Kim fixed her gaze on a pasture full of black-and-white cows to the right of the highway. "Of course, a honeymoon allows some bending of the rules."

"You'd better believe it." The lush green landscape all about them wasn't softening Gray's mood. "I'd like to keep right on driving."

"It's too bad that you didn't do it yesterday and skip Port Lathrop. Then none of this would have happened."

"If there's anything I can't stand, it's a Monday-morning quarterback," Gray snarled. "I didn't know that I was going to hit a combination of rundown smoke alarms as well as a rundown . . ." Too late, he decided that any more comments about rundown Victorian houses would hardly be diplomatic. He muttered something profane and then said, "The way this is going, we're at a knockdown-dragout and we aren't even married yet."

His doleful expression was so surprising that Kim burst out laughing. After an instant, Gray started to chuckle himself, his broad shoulders shaking.

"At least I had an excuse for not keeping that appointment at the port with Amherst," he managed to say. "It was a good thing, because I certainly couldn't have gotten any favors out of him today."

"Have you let the people you work for know what's happening?"

He shook his head. "They won't expect to hear from me over the weekend. I can check in at the first of the week and it'll be okay." He kept his tone casual as he changed the subject. "What does Gerald do?" Seeing her frown, he went on, "For a living, I mean."

"Oh, that."

Gray's slow smile showed again. "It does have its uses. For eating—among other things. Or does Gerald live on handouts from his father?"

"Certainly not." Kim brought her attention back from a bank of wild rhododendrons on her side of the road to go to Gerald's defense. "He's tried quite a few ways to make a living since he quit college. It isn't his fault if he's been plagued with bad luck. Take that plywood firm he invested in . . ." Her voice trailed off.

"What about it?" Gray prompted finally, when she made no attempt to break the silence between them.

She sighed. "Well, the foreign competition ruined the plywood market in this part of the world, and after about a year the company had to declare bankruptcy. I heard that the bank lost a bundle on it, and naturally that didn't make John very happy."

"Since he probably talked the other bank directors

into granting the loan to Gerald in the first place," Gray said, hazarding a guess.

Kim nodded, forgetting that he wasn't looking at her and then saying, "You're right," when he shot a quick glance her way. "Anyhow, after that Gerald didn't do much better. He tried selling for a while and then he invested in a gift shop. I understand that's doing quite well now."

"But you haven't been back in Port Lathrop long enough to be sure. Isn't that right?"

"It wouldn't matter if I'd only been back a day. The Elders told me all about it before they left town, and Ozzie gives me the latest commentary on his morning coffee break."

"You mean the carpenter?"

"Our one and only."

"Who's apt to spread this morning's doings, too. It's just as well we left town." Gray shrugged and accelerated. "Maybe when we get back all will be forgiven."

"I hope so." Kim rubbed her forehead fretfully and wished that her developing headache would take to its heels, as well. "Couldn't you have sent Carola on her way south before we left?"

"I tried." Gray's voice was grim. "God knows I tried. She insisted that a weekend at the Stratford was just what she needed to soothe her nerves. After she offered to house-sit for you, I couldn't very well show her the door."

"I see your point. There wasn't much time to explain things, but I imagine that Ozzie can answer most questions she has."

"You mean he wears more than one hat?"

She nodded. "He's also the resident house-sitter and security guard if we need him."

"Isn't he a little old for that?"

"He's tremendously loyal—that makes up for a lot."

"Some good deadbolt locks would help the cause along, too. Now what's so funny?" His last query came when she started to laugh helplessly.

"You are," she said, settling back again when she found that her headache wasn't improved by such exertions. "The way you go from smoke alarms to installing deadbolt locks within twenty-four hours. I warn you that the Stratford drives efficiency experts straight up the wall. It also plays havoc with bank accounts. I can testify to that."

"Then I'll just drop my bright ideas in the suggestion box when I leave."

That announcement brought an extra throbbing to Kim's temples. "And when's that going to be?" she asked, taking care to make her tone suitably casual.

"There's a little thing called a marriage ceremony to go through first." Gray's attention was straight ahead, intent on keeping a safe distance from the big truck and trailer taking up most of the winding two-lane road ahead of them. "Why in the devil doesn't he pull over on the shoulder?"

Kim was glad to see the truck driver eventually do just that as the road widened, allowing them and all the cars behind them to accelerate and pass. "About this marriage ceremony," she began hesitantly a little later.

"What about it?"

Gray's tone wasn't encouraging, but she persisted.

"Well, I just wondered what we're supposed to do during the waiting period."

"Stay out of sight."

"I *know* that," she said doggedly. "But where?"

"In the motel, I suppose." His mouth took on that grim line again. "I'm not an expert on this."

"I didn't mean that you were. I just thought we should lay down a few ground rules."

"Why don't you stop dancing around the maypole?" he said dryly. "You don't have to worry about sharing your bed—if that's what this is all about."

"Well, I do think we should discuss it. After all, we are two adults . . ."

"But not consenting ones."

"I beg your pardon?"

"You heard me." He shot her a sideways glance which didn't miss her flushed cheeks or downcast eyes. "How old did you say you were?" he rapped out.

"Twenty-three."

"Well, you're not acting like it," he said autocratically. "You didn't have any reason to complain about sharing a bed with me last night, did you?"

"But I didn't even know it."

"The important thing is that I *was* there."

"But you didn't know *I* was there," she countered, with the sinking knowledge that she was going to lose the argument. "At least, that's what you said."

"The hell I did. I didn't have a chance to say anything. Your friend Amherst did all the talking—if you'll remember."

"At this point, I'd have trouble spelling my name properly," she informed him. "What difference does it make now?"

"You're the one who brought up the subject."

"I did not. At least, I didn't mean to," she said, floundering and wondering who had started the argument. She rubbed her forehead again.

"What's the matter? Do you have a headache?"

Gray's terse questions made her blink and nod reluctantly.

"Do you have any aspirin with you?" he asked then.

"That won't help. It feels like a migraine that's settling in. I get them once in a while," she added apologetically.

Gray's eyebrows drew together and he looked grimmer than ever.

"It needn't change anything," Kim assured him. "I have some pills for it, and I'll take them when we get to the motel."

"It's not surprising that you're under the weather. I realize I haven't helped things by fighting back all the time. For what it's worth—I apologize. And you certainly don't have to worry about sharing any more bedrooms or beds with me. We'll get a suite, and that should serve the purpose for everybody."

"It sounds like a good solution," she told him, "but honestly, I wasn't worrying. You aren't the type to—to—"

"You'd better quit while you're ahead. I'm not sure whether it was a compliment, but I'll take it as read—considering you're feeling puny. Why don't you just put your head back and close your eyes until we arrive at the city hall. It won't do if you go in looking like a ghost—they'll think I've been beating you already."

She managed a grin. "Already? You've got me shivering in my shoes."

"That'll be the day," he said obliquely. "Close your eyes and be quiet."

"Yes, sir." She tried to find a comfortable spot against the side window for her head but wasn't too surprised when Gray's strong arm pulled her back against him. She surveyed his profile through half-closed lashes as he kept his gaze straight ahead. Her eyelids dropped down again and she settled onto his tweed-clad shoulder, strangely comforted by his presence.

She didn't plan to fall asleep and was surprised when she felt a gentle shake and Gray's voice saying softly, "Hey, wake up! You can't sleep all day."

She struggled upright, still only half conscious. "What's the matter? Oh, we're here!" The last came as she focused on the gray stone courthouse of Port Victor. It was a pleasantly ugly building constructed at the bottom of a steep hillside and facing out onto the gray-blue waters of the Strait of Juan de Fuca. She blinked again and then sat up, running her fingers through her hair. "It's not good enough," she said, with a critical look at her pale face in the sun-visor mirror. "I must have a comb somewhere. Where on earth did I put my purse?"

"Take it easy. We don't have to catch a plane or anything." Gray was looking at the old stone building in front of them. "That place has been around for a while. This town must be as old as Port Lathrop."

"The whole peninsula was settled years ago," Kim murmured as she tried to smooth her tousled hair.

Gray turned his attention to her, asking, "How do

you feel?" when she'd finished with her comb. "You still look awfully pale."

"The headache's better but it's still around," she admitted, knowing that it wouldn't help to lie to him. "Once I swallow my pills, I should be okay."

He nodded and reached for his door handle. "Well, this shouldn't take long. Unless the license clerk is still at lunch."

Fortunately he wasn't. And Kim felt a surge of relief when the man's glance passed casually over their application. It helped that she'd been working and living out of state until recently. Gray's address in Arizona also was blessedly anonymous as far as local interest went, and once he'd paid the license fee, the gray-haired clerk merely announced the deadline on the waiting period and went back to his desk without another glance.

"So far, so good," Gray murmured, holding the office door and ushering Kim ahead of him out into the hallway of the ancient building. "Any other detours, or shall we try our luck for a place to stay?"

Kim tried to ignore the throbbing in her temples as she said, "Let's go to the resort, if you don't mind. There's really only one good one in town."

"I think I saw it when we drove in. That big one on the water?"

She nodded. "I hope we don't have trouble getting space. It's great for conventions and people wanting to take the ferry trip to Vancouver Island."

Gray opened the glass courthouse door for her. "Conventions in this weather?" he wanted to know, jerking a thumb to indicate the gray overcast sky with clouds rolling in from the coast.

"In this part of the world, people don't stop breathing just for a little bit of rain," she told him tartly. "As a matter of fact, we have less precipitation than quite a few parts of northern California."

"Obviously, your Chamber of Commerce keeps that news well hidden. Don't worry about it," he added, seeing her mutinous expression. "You've convinced me, and you can hold a good thought for the resort. In the meantime, let's get in the car. Some of that Northern California rain took a wrong heading and I'm getting wetter than hell."

Kim waited in the car when they drove into the resort a few minutes later. Gray handed over their license application, saying, "You keep this. I'd hate to have it fall out of my pocket while I'm registering."

Kim nodded and scrunched back in the seat. There was no point in tempting fate; Port Victor wasn't that far from Port Lathrop, and right then she didn't want to run into any old school friends.

When Gray emerged from the office of the resort some five minutes later, she could see from the set expression on his face that something had gone amiss.

"Now what's wrong?" she asked, scarcely giving him time to get back behind the wheel.

"You were right about the conventions," he said, handing her the room key and switching on the ignition. "If we'd come much later, we'd have been out of luck entirely. As it is—no suites."

Kim's brows drew together. "You mean . . ."

"A double room, but they swear it's a *big* double room." He was pulling slowly down the big parking area as he checked the numbers on the resort doors. "I like the looks of this place with all that weathered gray shake and waterfront location. Maybe we landed on our feet after all."

Kim wasn't put off by his determined red herring. "Couldn't you have gotten two single rooms?"

Gray's pressure on the accelerator didn't increase, but his grasp on the steering wheel tightened visibly. "You seem to have forgotten the object of this maneuver. We're married, according to half the population of your hometown. I registered us as Mr. and Mrs. Stanton. Even in this liberated age, married couples stay in one room." The last came out tersely as he braked and pulled into one of the few available parking spaces by the bay wing of the resort.

"You don't have to be sarcastic."

"For God's sake, use your head, woman." He switched off the ignition and turned to face her on the seat. Then, seeing her drawn, ashen countenance, his aggressiveness faded as quickly as it had come. "Hell! I forgot you were under the weather."

"That doesn't give me an excuse for acting like an idiot," Kim confessed, reaching for her purse. "I keep forgetting my moves in this charade. Do you need help with the bags?"

He shook his head and handed her the room key. "Go on ahead and open our door. I'll be right behind you."

Kim was glad to find that the wide ground-floor hallway was deserted, allowing her to reach their room without passing any other guests on the way. She fumbled as she put the key in the lock and knew it was fortunate that she'd never contemplated an affair. She would probably sign the wrong name on the register with the manager looking on and forget to bring any luggage.

"Having trouble?" Gray had come up behind her and put down the bags.

"No, not really." She turned the knob and swung the door wide open to survey the interior. "Mmm—nice!" Her voice didn't waver, even when her gaze lingered on the two oversized beds which took up most of the room.

"It looks okay," Gray confirmed, bringing in the bags and putting them on two luggage racks in the commodious dressing room which adjoined an attractive bath. He followed her then into the main room, fiddling for a moment with the television set and finally going over to inspect the small contemporary fireplace near the sliding glass doors which led out onto a lanai.

It seemed important to keep moving, Kim thought, trying to look as if she inspected resort rooms all the time. Pinning a bright smile on her face, she managed to pull aside the balcony door and stepped outside. "We're right on the water," she added brightly. It wasn't necessary to make that announcement, she thought, even as she said it. Anyone with eyes in his head couldn't miss the expanse of water. At that moment, the waves lapped the shore with soft lady-like sibilance, but she knew that if the wind came up, they could be transformed to dangerous furies. The perfect setting for romance, she mused; a storm lashing outside while inside there'd be a fire in the fireplace and soft music as two people sat close together staring into the bright flames.

"Never the time and the place and the loved one altogether," Gray quoted, coming out on the lanai beside her.

"I—I—don't know what you mean," Kim stammered, horrified that he seemed to be reading her mind once again.

He stared down at her, his expression not giving anything away. " 'S funny—I could have sworn you would. You'd better shed some of those clothes and go lie down. If you ever expect to get rid of that headache," he added before she could protest.

"What are you going to do?"

"Damned if I know." His mouth quirked as he went over to survey the television schedule prominently displayed on the long bureau. "I'll find something."

Evidently he didn't plan to do anything drastic like leaving the room, Kim thought irritably, as she watched his tall immobile figure lounging against the television set, seemingly intent on the printed page. Well, if he thought she was going to ask him to leave he was crazy, she decided. The way her head was throbbing, she was beyond such subtleties. Without another word, she walked over to her suitcase and unearthed a pair of severely tailored cotton pajamas with a matching thigh-length robe. She went into the bathroom and changed behind the closed door. Not until she had folded her other clothes and had a hand on the doorknob did she relent and check her reflection in the mirror. She uttered a small moan of dismay as she saw her wraithlike color. Whatever had possessed her to buy a pair of pale-orchid pajamas, she thought in chagrin. Right then, she looked like a family ghost and a darned anemic one at that.

A sharp rap on the door and Gray's voice demanding, "Anything wrong in there?" prompted her to open it hurriedly.

"What makes you think there's anything wrong?" she repeated.

"I heard a groan."

"Oh, that." She started to gesture and remembered too late that she was clutching a handful of clothes. Hastily, she walked over and shoved them into her suitcase.

"Yes, that," he persisted, staying where he was.

"It wasn't anything. I just looked in the mirror—" That sentence stopped abruptly as she realized what she was saying.

"A very sensible outfit." His glance went over the pajamas quickly, although she knew he didn't miss an inch on the way. "What color are those—mauve?"

"Certainly not. Mauve is sort of a faded purple."

"Worn by elderly British women? It couldn't be mauve then, could it?"

As a putdown, it was superb, and, headache or no, Kim could have hit him over the head with the nearby ice bucket. She stifled the urge with difficulty and reached for her bottle of headache pills instead. "If you don't mind, I'll take these now."

"Good idea." He searched for a clean glass, carefully put an ice cube in it, and filled it with water before handing it to her. "Be my guest."

When he followed her into the main room a moment later, he stood by while she crawled onto the bed and then solicitously pulled a comforter over her feet. "Are you sure you wouldn't be more comfortable getting *into* bed?" he wanted to know.

"I'm fine," Kim snapped, wondering how he could be so infuriating without doing one thing wrong. "If you don't mind, I'll just ignore you for a few minutes until—"

"—the pills work," he finished for her. "That's the idea. I'll probably read or go for a walk. If you don't need me for anything."

"Not a thing," she managed to say, just as politely. It was remarkable considering that what she really wanted at that moment was to pull him down beside her on the bed and rest her head on his broad chest, relaxing in the comfort of his strong clasp. But instead, she had to lie in her teeth and close her eyes so that she wouldn't have to see any more of his carefully polite, impersonal gaze.

The treatment wasn't surprising, she told herself bitterly; if a woman persisted in wearing mauve—and there wasn't any other description for the color of her hateful pajamas—she deserved to be politely fobbed off by a man.

That conclusion was so loathsome that if she hadn't already had a miserable headache, she would have contracted one.

It was with difficulty that she kept from moaning again. Instead, she bit down on her lip and kept her eyes tightly closed—until the painkiller blessedly took effect.

Chapter Five

When Kim awakened the headache was gone. That was her first thought and the only clear-cut one. Other than a pleased awareness of relief from pain, her thoughts were still in the half-waking, half-drowsy stage, and she made no attempt to clear them. It was a pleasant plateau that she occupied; she was aware of the soft murmur of the water which came with measured regularity against the shore, and occasionally the sound of gulls crying as they gathered on the city pier down the block. Her half-closed glance discovered there wasn't a glimmer of sunlight at the window, so an overcast was still shrouding the port.

Not that it truly mattered. There wasn't anything to really bother her just then except for an intrusive hum that sounded steadily—just barely loud enough to be heard with her head in the pillow. It couldn't be a fly, she told herself. Not at that time of the year! She closed her eyes again and finally identified it as the climate-control thermostat over her bed. The gentle breeze of warm air settling down on her showed that it was turned to the heat cycle rather than cooling air conditioning.

Her brows drew together as that thought registered and her eyes came wide open as other memories blotted out her euphoria. This wasn't a family weekend in Port Victor—far from it! Not with Gray Stanton sharing her bedroom.

She pushed up hastily on her elbow just as his voice came across from where he sat stretched out in a chair by the balcony. "I wondered when you were going to surface."

She rubbed her eyes to clear the sleep from them and caught a glimpse of her mauve pajama sleeve in the process. It was enough to make her slump back against the headboard as all the other disturbing elements of the day came to mind.

"Still aching, is it?" There was concern in Gray's voice as he got to his feet and came over to the side of the mattress to stare down at her.

Kim blinked, trying to figure out what he meant, and then she said hurriedly, "Oh, my headache. No, it's gone, praise be."

His own brows drew together. "You looked so unhappy I thought—never mind, it doesn't matter."

"I'm just slow if I take a nap during the day," she explained, wishing that she didn't look like somebody in a winding sheet. She knew instinctively he was accustomed to seeing another type of woman in such intimate surroundings. Then, making a project out of pushing back the coverlet and swinging her legs to the floor, she asked, "Have you been here long?"

He shrugged, keeping his glance on her steadily. "Long enough. Do you feel like eating?"

"Now that you mention it, it's just what I do feel like. Can you give me a few minutes to change?"

"Well, I didn't expect you to make a grand entrance at the dining room in those." He shoved his hands in his pockets and stepped back so that she could maneuver past him. "Especially since we don't want to attract any more attention than necessary."

As if her pajamas would raise an eyebrow even if she lingered by the ice machine in the corridor, Kim thought, searching through her suitcase for something attractive to wear. The casual pants outfit was out—somehow Gray had found time to change into a crisp white shirt to go with his herringbone sport jacket and charcoal slacks.

Her hand hesitated over a red polyester dress which she knew would be wrinkle-free and came with a nicely fitting off-white suede vest which had brought her compliments in the past. Along with a pair of high-heeled red leather pumps, she should look halfway decent.

"Very nice," was all Gray said when she emerged from the bathroom a little later on, but she noticed that his gaze went from the top of her head down to those red leather pumps with thorough masculine appraisal, and he made no attempt to hide it. Kim decided suddenly that two could play at that game and took the opportunity to do a little staring herself. Although Gray was his usual immaculate self, there was a tension on his face that hadn't been there before. His expression wasn't conducive to questions or comments, so she followed meekly when he opened the hall door and said, "We'd better get moving to make our dinner reservation."

Kim nodded and caught up her purse as she left the room. She recalled from previous visits that there were covered walkways in the resort, so the light mist which still enveloped Port Victor didn't bother them as they went from their wing to the main section housing the dining room.

She'd thought earlier that Gray wasn't the type of person to be intimidated by maître d's and wasn't surprised to find they were shown to a choice, secluded window table even though the popular eating place was jammed with patrons.

"This isn't much of a holiday for you," Gray said when they were seated and studying their menus. "Apparently Victoriana is the preferred decor in this part of the world."

"Only the furniture is the same," she told him solemnly. "Fortunately the food bears little resemblance to the Stratford."

"Last night wasn't a fair test. I promise to keep an open mind when you're not faced with a power failure. How about the Dungeness crab? Or has that migraine left you without any appetite?"

Surprised that he was so knowledgeable about such things, Kim lowered her menu. "Actually, I'm not terribly hungry." Her lips quirked. "I'd order an omelet except it might bring back too many horrible memories for you."

"Try a nice broiled steak instead," he said, putting down his own menu with the economy of motion to which she had become accustomed. "You need some calories and red meat if you're going to keep on fighting back."

Kim relaxed and smiled. "Fair enough. You can make all the vital decisions this time."

While they were waiting to be served their vichyssoise as an appetizer, Gray's glance rested on an intricate mahogany sideboard nearby which was in keeping with the deep-red velvet drapes at the windows and intricate brass chandeliers casting subdued light over the room. "Some of these furnishings look like the real thing," he said. "I suppose a decorator decided a little authenticity would add to the place. Like that sideboard, for instance."

Kim nodded and gave the sideboard a thoughtful look. "Probably that piece originally had one of those monstrous mirrors and all sorts of geegaws so there wasn't much demand for it."

"Not unless you have a barn-sized dining room." Gray took a sip of water and idly traced a circle around the base of the goblet. "I noticed that the Stratford has some pretty choice pieces of furniture. That settee by the fireplace and that sideboard thing up in your bedroom."

Kim leaned back so that their waiter could deposit the iced cups of vichyssoise and waited until he'd left before she said solemnly, "Actually 'that sideboard thing' is a 'butler's secretary' and it's worth a bundle, but I'd happily change it for a decent bureau with big drawers. That shows what a heathen I am."

"Hardly. I'd just say you were expressing a feminine prerogative."

"A habit of mine," she acknowledged.

There was only idle conversation for the rest of the meal after that. Gray seemed content to enjoy his food, and Kim was surprised to find how good the broiled steak and baked potato tasted. When she finally had finished and refused dessert, choosing to linger over her coffee instead, Gray said, "You could do with a few extra courses. Even with that bright-red dress as camouflage, you're a ways from fighting fit. What have you been doing to yourself?"

"You mean—other than what happened today?"

He nodded coolly. "You looked on the fragile side yesterday when I first saw you."

"And here I thought I was the epitome of a well-organized landlady." When he didn't rise to that, she shrugged. "I've been trying to figure out how to get the Stratford into black ink, and it's been a worry for months. The renovating and refurbishing have run way over the estimates—even after I was lucky enough to buy some pieces from the Amhersts."

Gray's eyes narrowed and he shoved his coffee cup aside. "Like what?"

She smiled, amused at his blunt question. "Like the butler's secretary. It originally came from their family home, but they'd had it in storage for years. The market for such pieces was limited and they decided to sell it. By then, Gerald needed money to get his shop into a healthy financial condition. As a matter of fact, the whole town's economy is shaky right now. Everybody wants to save our historical landmarks, but it helps if you have a million dollars or so to pay the bills. At least the Amhersts had the good sense to sell out years ago and move into a modern house up on the bluff overlooking the Strait."

"Well, Gerald's not tending the home fires tonight. No—don't turn around," Gray cautioned, keeping his own head lowered. "He's just going into the bar with a man. Unless you're hell-bent on renewing your friendship right now—"

"You know I'm not," she interrupted fiercely.

"Okay then." He looked over her shoulder again and nodded. "It's safe. They've disappeared. From what I saw," he added, "Gerald has already been hitting the bottle, so I hope he doesn't plan to drive back to Port Lathrop tonight." Seeing her puzzled look, he asked, "Now what's the matter?"

"I just wondered why he's here. He didn't say

anything about driving this far, and the weekend's a busy time for his shop."

"Well, from his expression, it didn't look like strictly a social occasion." Gray gestured to a passing waiter and requested the check. He waited until the man had gone to get it before turning back to Kim. "You didn't let it slip to Gerald that you'd be here, did you?"

"Of course not. Besides, when did I have time? You've been riding herd on me all day."

"I thought it was called 'keeping company,' " Gray said mildly.

When the check arrived he looked it over and signed, adding some bills for the tip. "Let's go before Gerald comes out again. There's no use pressing our luck." A minute later when he was shepherding her from the dining room he said, "On second thought, you go on ahead. There's something I want to do."

She shot an anxious glance toward the adjoining bar, where Gerald and his friend had apparently gone. "You're not going to get into trouble, are you?"

"You don't have to hold my hand," Gray started to say and then took a deep breath as he saw her concerned expression. "Just give me a few minutes. Here—you'll need our room key. And don't hang around the lobby."

"I thought I might find a traveling salesman to help fill my free time," she countered sweetly. "You take away all the fun."

Gray administered a sharp slap to her derrière before she could get beyond reach. "You must be feeling better. It was easier when you were under the weather. Get going, will you?"

Without waiting to see if she followed his dictate,

he went around the corner into the shadowed bar, where candles in red hurricane lamps on the tables provided the only illumination.

Kim frowned after him, but turned obediently toward the walkway which led back to their wing. She *was* feeling better, but still not strong enough to have argued further or deliberately disobeyed—however much she resented Gray's authoritarian manner. He was right about one thing—she certainly didn't want to run into Gerald at that moment and have to parry any more embarrassing questions.

The sound of footsteps near an exit door in the corridor made her draw in her breath sharply as she caught a glimpse of a young woman with long brown hair who disappeared into the darkened parking area. Surely Carola wasn't at the resort, too! Kim chewed on her lip as she thought about it. The other woman could have driven up with Gerald or, what was even more disconcerting, arrived at Gray's invitation.

As Kim considered that possibility, she realized that it wouldn't take much more before her headache came back with a vengeance. She muttered a fervent "Damnation!" and started on her way again.

She lingered in their corridor to fill a bucket of ice at the machine before going back to the room. Once she'd closed the door behind her, she looked with sudden loathing at the comfortable surroundings and put down the ice with such force that one cube spilled out and slithered onto the carpet.

Having to retrieve it from under the edge of her bed didn't improve her temper. She opened the balcony door and tossed the melting cube into the low shrubbery which separated the building from the narrow rocky beach at the edge of the Strait. She rubbed the dampness from her hand idly as she stared out across the black waters, barely able to make out the lights of a freighter which moved far out in the channel. Aside from a few scattered spot-lights on the city pier to her left where the Canadian ferry was berthed, there was nothing to disturb the inky darkness. Moonlight shimmered occasionally when the heavy clouds parted or thinned under the scudding Chinook wind. Kim shivered, wrapping her arms across her breast as a sudden gust swept the balcony. There was no point in catching cold just because of her reluctance to go back into that empty room, she told herself. Another gust which rattled the shrubbery convinced her, and she left the balcony, pulling the glass door closed and drawing the long drape across it.

For an instant she thought about putting a match to the logs in the small fireplace, then decided against it. If Gray found a crackling fire and soft music on the radio, he'd be more suspicious than ever. She sat down on the edge of her bed and then got up to survey the television schedule, sighing as she saw the selection. She wasn't in the mood for a spaghetti western or the two-hour drama which promised violence, drugs, and illicit love behind prison bars. "Another happy night of prime time," she muttered in disgust and decided to go to bed.

There was no way of knowing when Gray would return, and it would save embarrassment all around if he found her asleep. It had been hard enough to find safe conversational topics during dinner; he cer-tainly wouldn't want to discuss the weather for the rest of the night.

Her careful planning was doomed when she heard

a key rattle in the door some twenty minutes later. Kim had lingered in front of the mirror after she'd donned the hated pajamas, wondering whether she should put on a light application of lipstick. A well-scrubbed feminine look might be organic and the latest thing, but when combined with faded cotton pajamas, it made her look as if she were rehearsing for her funeral.

The sudden sound of Gray's presence prompted her to drop the lipstick as if it were red-hot. She dashed around the corner of the dressing room and made a determined leap for her bed. As the door opened, she was still trying frantically to get under the covers.

"What's with the squirrel act?"

Gray's question caught her on her knees. "I don't know what you mean," she countered breathlessly. "I was just getting into bed."

"You could have fooled me—I thought you were trying to bury nuts in the mattress with all that scrabbling."

"Don't be ridiculous." She felt a little more in command as she arranged a pillow against the headboard. "How did you get in? I thought you gave me the key."

He dangled one from his fingers. "Duplicate. All you have to do is ask the desk clerk. Two people—two keys." He dropped it on the bureau then and laid a newspaper alongside. "Why the big rush to get in bed?"

Kim opened her lips to answer and realized that it was a "when did you quit beating your wife" type of question. No matter what she said, she was in trouble.

Gray used the interval to go over and perch on the

edge of his own bed and subject her to another raking appraisal. "Those pajamas couldn't have been the temptation," he said finally.

"What's wrong with them?"

"Not one goddamned thing." He stood up suddenly and went across to sit in an upholstered chair by the window. "I suppose you thought you'd get safely tucked away in bed before I came back on the scene. You needn't have worried."

"It never entered my mind." She kept her glance averted so he wouldn't see through that whopper. "Anyhow, I thought I saw Carola on my way back to the room, so I didn't know when to expect you."

He frowned at that. "You couldn't have seen her."

"Oh? Why do you say that?"

"Because I phoned her at the Stratford this afternoon while you were sleeping. She didn't mention anything about leaving."

"It's possible that she might have done it on the spur of the moment—especially if she thought she had a chance of seeing you again."

Kim knew her last comment would annoy him, and she felt a surge of perverse pleasure when she saw his mouth tighten. "That migraine must have addled your thinking," he said in an ominous level tone. "Give me one good reason why my brother's fiancée would be following me around."

"She *did* appear at the Stratford this morning," Kim replied, pulling the sheet primly up to her waistline as she spoke.

"That's different."

Her eyebrows went up. "If you say so."

"I certainly do," he flared. "You must have a great idea of my morals—making accusations like that."

"I merely made a statement. You're the one who's getting hot under the collar."

"Well, unless you want me to get a lot more unpleasant, I'd suggest that we change the subject," he told her with finality. "Will it bother you if I turn on the television?"

"No, of course not." She bit her lips, trying to decide whether to be fobbed off like that, and then decided against it. "I thought you were going to tell me what happened in the bar," she said, as he got up and started over to turn on the set.

His expression didn't give anything away as he stopped and turned to face her across the room. "What makes you think anything did?"

"Because you wouldn't have gone in there otherwise. Did you talk to Gerald?"

"Lord, no." Gray moved over to the bureau and rested one hip on the edge of it, evidently deciding to humor her. "I went to a great deal of trouble to stay out of sight. Fortunately, there was a pay-phone enclosure just around the corner from him and his friend, so I had an excuse."

"To eavesdrop?"

"Don't sound so shocked." He looked amused suddenly. "You're not the only one who has a misguided imagination. If Gerald was unhappy about your default, he hid it well. From what I could hear, he was getting smashed for another reason entirely."

Kim made a small sound of annoyance. "You didn't have to play detective for that information. Gerald was just a good friend of mine."

"That wasn't the way he sounded this morning."

"Well, you can see that his passion didn't last long," Kim said dryly, settling back against her pillow.

"If I know Gerald, he was talking business tonight."

Gray pursed his lips thoughtfully. "You're right. Do you free-lance on the side with a crystal ball?"

"Hardly. I know that he goes on buying trips all the time," she said, pleased that Gray was looking on her with approval for the first time since he'd entered the room. As he slowly shook his head then, she shrugged. "No? What other kind of business is there?"

"He wasn't buying. Apparently he'd been selling— only his chum had neglected to come across with the payoff. Gerald was threatening all kinds of mayhem if he didn't get the money."

"And?" Kim asked impatiently when Gray paused.

"Well, from what I could overhear, the fellow said that he was expecting his cash flow to improve." Gray grinned at her look of disdain. "His words, not mine. He mentioned a sale at Haymarket tomorrow. Wherever that is."

"Victoria. In Canada. On Vancouver Island—at the other end of the ferry run," Kim said tersely.

"I have heard of it," Gray informed her solemnly. "And what about Haymarket?"

"It's a big antique mart. Tomorrow's their weekly sale day. I wonder what Gerald sold him."

"I didn't have time to hang around any longer and find out," Gray confessed. "Somebody came up to use the phone about then, and I couldn't make my imaginary conversation last any longer."

Her lips quirked. "You weren't getting the right answers. You should have called here and let me supply the missing links."

"I wasn't sure you'd want to get in the game. What's the matter?" The last came when he saw her grimace and suddenly rub her neck.

"Nothing—at least not much. I must have just pulled a muscle. It's all right," she said hurriedly as she saw him get to his feet and start toward her. "I'm sure it will go away."

"Maybe I can hurry it along." He sat down on the edge of her mattress and reached for her shoulders. "This will work better if you slide around and turn your back to me."

"It isn't necessary. Well, really!" she protested when he took her under the arms and turned her around without ceremony.

"Now, hold still," he instructed. "Is this the place?"

The feel of his strong fingers kneading her tense shoulder muscles was so good that Kim forgot all about fighting her lost cause. "Mmmm," she approved breathlessly. "Maybe up a little on the left."

"Show me where."

Silently she followed his instructions and then tried to relax as he gently worked his way around the base of her neck and out toward the end of her shoulders. Kim was enjoying the feeling of his fingers so much that she wasn't quite sure when the massage moved down and around, but the soft stroke of those same fingers along the side of her breast made her inhale sharply. "That's enough, thanks," she said breathlessly, pulling away to face him from the headboard. "I feel fine now."

"You don't look it. For my money, it will take more than a little therapeutic massage to help your cause along."

She attempted to draw the sheet up higher as she sat there so that he couldn't see the way her heart was thundering against the thin material of her pajamas. "I suppose you could manage to supply whatever's missing," she said scornfully.

"I imagine so." A ghost of a smile lit his face as he reached over to trace a firm finger down her hot cheek and then let it continue its deliberate path down the front of her pajamas.

He left a trail of fire on her skin, and it was all Kim could do to sit there and not lean across the few inches that separated them as he brought his hand finally to rest on her thigh.

The intimate touch made her stare wide-eyed at him. "You promised," she managed to whisper finally when the silence and tension grew.

"That was a long time ago. There's nothing that says we can't change the house rules. After all, if we're going to share a marriage license for a few months, we could share some other things as well."

His cold statement brought Kim to her senses as effectively as tipping the ice bucket over her head. "No thanks," she said, moving her leg out from under his clasp in a way that didn't need explaining. "A little casual lovemaking doesn't appeal to me—it never has."

His glance hardened, but he didn't change his tone. "You might like it."

"With a good teacher?"

His color rose under her derisive look. "I don't carry around references, but there haven't been many complaints."

"I'll bet there haven't," she countered, with a clear picture of Carola in her mind's eye. During the confrontation in the bedroom of the Stratford, that young woman had showed that she could still change Stanton brothers with the slightest encouragement. Even the thought made Kim's stomach muscles tighten, and she looked shakily back at Gray. "I'll take my post-graduate training with someone else."

"Don't be a damned little fool." He pulled her across his lap, adding, "You don't know what you're talking about," before he brought his mouth down fiercely on hers.

After an instant of stunned surprise, Kim struggled to get free. She knew that she'd be utterly lost if she surrendered the slightest bit under Gray's determined persuasion. Then a moment later, when his lips hardened and savaged hers to respond, she found that trying to pretend she was unaffected was the most difficult thing she'd done in her life. Every instinct and desire urged her to abandon her defenses and capitulate to his masculine strength.

"Wake up, damn you," he growled and shook her slightly when she continued to resist.

Her lips parted reluctantly, then her clenched fingers opened against his chest and went up to smooth his thick hair—gently stroking his head instead of trying to push it away. There was a thundering in her ears as she felt his hands move aside the last barrier between them.

Then—suddenly—it was all over. Whether Gray became annoyed with her shy response or simply tired of his experiment she'd never know. She *did* know that one minute the two of them were sharing a pillow while occupying a very narrow strip of the bed—and the next, he had pulled away and was getting unconcernedly to his feet. He didn't make any comment on her disheveled state, but the way he reached down and jerked the sheet back up over her spoke volumes.

"I didn't mean to let things get so far out of hand," he said finally, "but I'm damned if I'll apologize. You deserved that and more." His jaw was rock-hard as he lingered by the side of the bed, staring down at her.

"Thanks very much."

It was all Kim could do to keep her voice steady as she met his gaze, wondering why she'd thought that he would have been swept away by the magic of that kiss and left breathless—the way that she had. "If you think that I'm going to spend the next day or so being chased around the bedroom whenever you feel like some extracurricular fun and games . . ." she began.

"Oh, for God's sake, drop it, will you!" Gray kneaded the muscles at the back of his neck as if he'd suddenly contracted her headache and wasn't happy about it. "From now on, you're as safe as houses as far as I'm concerned. We'll play it by the book—your book. Whatever you choose to do with Gerald is your business."

His last careless comment made her wince inwardly. "That's kind of you," she responded, managing to sound as if she'd only been waiting for his seal of approval. "Naturally the same applies to your outside interests. I'd hate to have this arrangement cramp your style."

"And I thought you were such a shy little thing," he said, making no attempt to hide his annoyance. "Is there anything else you'd like to get off your chest, or shall we call it quits for the night?"

"That's all I have to say."

"Good." Her tremulous expression made him frown and add, "There's no use looking as if it's the end of the world. Get some sleep," he said roughly as he started for the door.

"Where are you going?" The words were out before Kim could stop them.

"Out." Gray paused with his hand on the knob. "And you don't have to worry when I come back. Right now, I could write a book on the advantages of monastic life."

Kim winced as the door slammed behind him.

If Gray's scathing expression was a barometer of his return, he wouldn't be back until the wee small hours. Kim leaned against her pillow and chewed on a knuckle as she wondered how she'd ever get reconciled to a marriage of convenience with the tall man who'd just slammed out of the room. Even the two days left before they could officially tie the knot loomed like a vast Sahara in front of her. It would be a wonder if they both made it to the altar unbruised and still speaking!

What was it the license clerk had called their three-day waiting stipulation? A "cooling-off time," that was it.

Suddenly she started to laugh, because the phrase was so apt. Things had cooled off, all right. If they got much colder, her prospective bridegroom would be pounding on the door of the city hall first thing in the morning demanding a refund on his license fee.

Chapter Six

It was a determined knocking on the hall door which finally awakened Kim the next morning.

Struggling up on one elbow, she squinted to see the bedside clock and gasped to discover that it was almost nine. Another series of knocks from the doorway made her call out, "Just a minute—I'm coming," and reach for her robe. Then, like a comic from the silent-picture era, she did a sudden double-take as her glance swept the empty bed near the window. The spread wasn't even rumpled and the extra blanket was still in exact folds at the end of the bed. So Gray hadn't come back at all during the night!

She was trying to assimilate that discouraging fact as she stumbled toward the doorway, tying the belt of her robe en route.

"Good morning, Mrs. Stanton." A cheerful young waiter stood with a room-service cart beside him. "I have your breakfast. Where would you like it?"

Kim tried to smooth her hair as she automatically stood aside to let him wheel the cart into the room. "Are you sure that's my breakfast? I don't remember ordering any."

"Mr. Stanton put the order in earlier," he told her,

pulling up beside the table next to the balcony. "Will this be all right?"

"Yes, of course." She tried to sound casual as she asked, "You mean this morning?"

He nodded, intent on transferring the silver coffee pot and a juice glass ensconced in a bed of ice cubes. "When he was in the coffee shop having his own breakfast earlier. I took the order myself."

"I see." She watched him arrange the silver and make a final check to see that everything was in place before wheeling the cart toward the door again. "Shall I sign the check or anything?"

"It's all taken care of. Whenever you're finished, just leave the tray outside in the hallway." He smiled at her over his shoulder. "Enjoy your breakfast."

Kim nodded and waited until the door had closed behind him before she cast another unhappy look at the food on the table. Since Gray had already eaten, it was useless to expect that he might put in a belated arrival for a second cup of coffee. As she walked into the dressing room to wash and brush her teeth, the sight of an envelope propped against her cosmetic kit brought her to a halt.

His note was written on the resort notepaper and was painfully direct. "Catching the morning ferry to Victoria to see the Haymarket auction rather than just marking time in Port Victor. You'll probably appreciate a day to yourself."

As a touching piece of correspondence it ranked right along with an annual reminder from her dentist, Kim thought bitterly.

She went back out to survey her breakfast with distaste. Her solitary breakfast, she reminded herself as she sipped the orange juice and took a silver cover off heated sweet rolls flanked by a rasher of bacon. The appetizing smell made her slide into the chair without wasting any more time. It was silly to stop eating just because Gray found better things to do with his day than stare at four walls of the resort with his intended.

Later, after she'd showered and dressed, she decided that Gray wasn't the only one who could plan an interesting day. She ruthlessly buried the fact that she would have loved a ferry trip to Victoria and an afternoon at the antique auction even though both were familiar territory. Certainly wild horses wouldn't drag that admission from her when Gray came back. Instead, she'd be full of enthusiasm about *her* day, she told herself, and almost believed it.

The time moved like molasses when she finally set out to wander around the town. Fortunately, the shops were open; weekends meant visitors and profits for Port Victor merchants even in early spring. Everybody was in on the act, except the weatherman, Kim thought, and he seemed determined to provide a thick cloud cover whenever the sun was tempted to shine through. A glimpse across the Strait showed that Vancouver Island was getting even blacker clouds, and Kim was human enough to hope that Gray might have forgotten to take a raincoat along.

Two days ago she wouldn't have harbored such uncharitable ideas, but her feminine pride was smarting over the unceremonious way he'd deserted her.

She kept a lookout as she window-shopped through the center of town. With Gray among the missing, she had no desire for a face-to-face encounter with Gerald. Explaining a honeymoon without a bridegroom was beyond her just then, and she'd certainly lost the dewy-eyed glow that brides were supposed to have.

She lingered in front of a shop window to survey her reflection and tried a practice smile to fit the occasion. An instant later, she felt like a fool when a bearded young man inside the store invitingly smiled back at her and started making his way through the browsers to the door.

"Oh, Lord," Kim muttered and fled into the next shop, pushing past some startled shoppers to get out of sight of the display window and finally hiding behind a curtained dressing room.

"Was there something special you wanted, miss?" It was a hard-faced sales woman who marched to the back of the shop to frown accusingly at Kim over the counter.

"No—I mean, yes, I think so." Kim looked around to see where she'd taken refuge and found a tantalizing display of feminine lingerie draped on hangers and languid mannequins around her. The closest one was wearing a sapphire satin gown and negligee set trimmed with matching lace. Compared to some of the other creations it was discreetly provocative, and compared to the pair of mauve pajamas currently reposing in her suitcase it was pure dynamite. "That outfit—the blue one," she said, waggling a finger toward the set in question. "Is it my size?"

The shopkeeper's severe expression was transformed as if by magic. "I think so," she said with an appraising glance over Kim's measurements. "I'll take it off the display. If you'd like to go into the dressing room . . ."

Kim cautiously poked her head around the curtained booth to see the bearded man from next door on the edge of the sidewalk, peering up the street. Another five minutes should do it, she decided and twitched the curtain aside.

It was closer to ten when she emerged with the gown and negligee clutched in her hand. "They fit beautifully," she admitted to the clerk. "I'll take them."

"We have a petticoat and bra in the same shade if you'd like to coordinate your ensemble," the woman said smoothly. "It's been very popular."

"No, thanks. This will do it." A glimpse of the price tags when she'd tried the outfit on had made Kim shudder. Any more indulgences and she'd need more than the Stratford's construction loan to get her through the month.

Nevertheless, she was in a better mood when she emerged from the shop with her purchase under her arm. Her bearded admirer had given up, and she made her way to a popular bayfront fish restaurant without any other detours.

She sat at the counter and ordered clam chowder, shaking her head afterward when the waitress urged dessert. By the time she'd finished and emerged from the restaurant there was a pale overlay of sunlight on the water. Umbrellas had disappeared, she noticed on her walk back to the resort, and while the town's tourists weren't shedding jackets or coats, there was a noticeably festive air in the shopping district.

The improved weather should make Gray's return ferry trip even more pleasant than usual, Kim thought. Her spirits were high and she was planning how she could casually appear in her new gorgeous blue creation as she finally reached her room and inserted the key. The phone started ringing as the door swung open, and she made a dive for the receiver, dropping her purchases on the bed as she passed.

"Kim?"

It was Gray's voice in the receiver, and his terse tone made her heart sink. "Yes," she got out breathlessly and then asked, "Where are you?"

"Still in Victoria. Along with a hundred or so other people."

"You mean you missed the ferry?"

"Hell, no! It's here, too. Some trouble with the boiler. They're hoping to get it repaired by morning."

"Then you'll have to . . ."

"Spend the night here? That's the latest report." There was a pause when she didn't reply and he went on in a softer voice, "I'm sorry. This development never occurred to me. Are you okay?"

"Just fine." Unwittingly a trace of sarcasm crept into her words and she went on brightly before he could comment on it. "My headache's gone completely."

"That's good."

"Certainly an improvement." *All we need now is another discussion of the weather,* she thought despairingly. That possibility prompted her to say quickly, "I haven't seen hide nor hair of Gerald."

"It's not surprising. I spent most of my time here dodging him. He was still drinking on the ferry this morning and had a seat in the front row at the auction this afternoon. I don't know why—he didn't do any bidding."

"Did he collect his money? That's a silly question," she added before he could. "They wouldn't be counting it out in front of everybody, would they?"

"They didn't, at any rate. Although his chum must

have collected plenty. There was certainly a mob at the auction."

"I know. There usually is."

Gray must have felt her unspoken rebuke, or perhaps he'd realized that leaving one's intended to cool her heels for a day wasn't usually done. At least not if he hoped for improved relations in the future. He cleared his throat and said, "I'm sorry about all this. If there are any more delays in the morning, I'll charter a plane."

Kim noted that he wasn't making any magnanimous gestures to get back right away. Not that she expected him to, of course.

"There's no rush," she said, managing to sound as if it didn't matter one way or the other. "We have one more day of the waiting period left to go."

"I know." The silence lengthened again until he said finally, "I hope you'll get some rest tonight."

There wasn't anything she could say to that. What did he think she was going to do? Kim wondered rebelliously. Hang out in the bar and see what was available? It was a pity she hadn't chatted with the bearded man on the sidewalk. At least that report would have livened up the conversation.

"I'll see you tomorrow then," Gray said, obviously tired of filling in the conversational gaps. "Incidentally, if you need to reach me tonight, I'll be at the Empress."

"I'll remember," Kim promised, knowing she wouldn't get in touch even if a tidal wave threatened or St. Helens erupted again. "Thanks for calling. Goodnight." She hung up before he could reply.

After that, it was a temptation to rent a car and drive back through the darkness to Port Lathrop. Kim chewed on her lip as she thought about all the possibilities and then decided against it. As long as she owned the Stratford and her parents summered in the town, she couldn't ignore the social conventions. There might be all sorts of new life-styles in other parts of the country, but Port Lathrop's citizens held firm to their traditional ideas—right or wrong.

The trouble was that she didn't want to be grateful to Gray for agreeing to follow the conventions. Nor did it make sense to indulge in a short-term affair with him just because they were going to share a marriage license. What she wanted was . . .

Her eyes widened as it occurred to her exactly what she *did* want at that moment, and an instant later she sighed as she realized that she didn't have one chance in a million of getting her wish. There wasn't a glass slipper and Gray hadn't mentioned love. Not once. Physical desire was fine for a weekend idyll, but it didn't rank with cherishing "in sickness and in health" for the long run.

The worst part was that she was old-fashioned, too, Kim thought. That meant getting through the next few days was going to be a major headache that would make her migraine of the day before seem like child's play.

She should be pleased that she had the chance of another night alone, she told herself as she packed away her gorgeous purchase in her suitcase. After a light dinner in the coffee shop, she'd plan what she'd do with her free time the next day.

She saw a placard by the registration desk that advertised a tour to the Game Farm down the peninsula. She'd heard favorable reports about the place even before Gray had mentioned that his brother planned to do some filming there. The tour left the resort at nine a.m.—that was earlier than the ferry could dock at Port Victor if they left Canada without further delays.

Kim signed up and paid for her ticket without any more hesitation, assuring the resort's hostess that she'd be in the lobby at the assigned time.

As she walked away, ticket in hand, a smile of satisfaction lingered on her lips. This time it would be Gray who discovered the note in their room and *he* could spend the day cooling his heels.

The next morning found her boarding the tour bus wearing navy-blue wool slacks and a cashmere cowled sweater. A suede jacket of lighter blue topped the casual outfit. She'd stuffed her room key and money in a clutch purse and slipped a foulard silk scarf in her jacket pocket.

The tour bus was only half full, and she managed a seat to herself near the middle. As they pulled out of the resort's parking lot, she peered across the Strait toward Vancouver Island and noticed a blob out on the water. Apparently she'd timed it right; by the time Gray's ferry docked, she'd be well out of town.

She settled back in her seat and opened the brochure which the tour-bus driver had handed out. The Game Farm had been captivating all comers for over thirty years, she discovered, and she looked at the pictures of four-footed inmates, trying to whip up her enthusiasm for the visit. Certainly there were enough animals to intrigue anybody—rhinos and yaks, bears and bisons. According to another section of the brochure, Scott Stanton's film crew would be just one of many who had used the premises. Kim read the list of feature pictures which had been made on the grounds and was impressed by the titles.

With so much in store, she thought that the bus driver and tour guide would head straight for the feature attraction, but the tour company apparently believed in showing visitors the entire countryside first. That included a detour past a small sawmill and a long lecture about the importance of lumbering to the peninsula. After that, there was a pleasant drive along the shoreline and a short stop at a crabbing pier where three berthed fishing boats were extolled to the amazement and, Kim suspected, amusement of their crews. By then, it was time for coffee, according to the tour director, and the bus pulled up in front of a small café which apparently existed on the morning and afternoon tour visitors. Kim took her coffee in a plastic cup and drank it outside, looking over the attractive vista provided by the gray-blue waters of the Strait and the sand spit which extended like a crooked finger toward the Canadian border.

Finally the group was herded aboard once again, and this time the director announced that the Game Farm was next. However, since their bus was too large to provide a firsthand look at the animals, they would be decanted into smaller vans when they arrived. Kim took a deep breath and told herself that it was fortunate she'd planned to spend the whole day touring, because she was certainly going to get her money's worth. For an instant, she let herself wonder what was happening back at the resort. Probably Gray had read her note and was congratulating himself that he'd earned another free day without struggling to find an excuse for it.

She was jolted back to the present when the bus driver braked strongly and turned off the ignition. "Here we are, ladies and gentlemen," the tour guide announced with professional cheer. "Everybody out, please." By then Kim suspected that he would have announced a list of plague victims with the same determined enthusiasm.

Much more goodwill and I'll lose my mind, Kim thought to herself as she gathered her purse and started down the aisle.

The tour guide was in his glory now that they'd reached the star attraction. "This way, Miss Cosgrove," he said, helping her down the bus steps with exaggerated care. "We'll all go over to the observation tower as soon as you take your places—then we'll distribute the bread."

"But we've just had coffee," Kim felt obliged to point out.

"The bread is for the animals," he told her with a superior smirk that made her want to trip him as he walked away. "This way, ladies and gentlemen—watch the steps please. Go right up to the observation platform, where you can view the route we'll be touring later. I'll see if our vans are on the way."

His passengers obediently filed up a set of rough log steps to a deck on the observation platform, which overlooked the entire Game Farm, spread out over some forty acres in the valley beneath them. The vista made Kim forget her momentary annoyance as she leaned against the sturdy railing, staring down at the animals in their individual compounds. Some species were caged, but the majority were in open grass pens or grazing at will in the far pastures. Only the rhinos seemed to have a sturdy enclosure, she decided and wondered how they managed to keep a colony of grizzly bears from roaming with a flimsy wire fence around their field. No wonder they had posted DO NOT LEAVE YOUR CAR signs all over the visitors' platform.

A honking from the parking lot made her turn to see their guide in the front of the big bus, gesturing for them to come. Three small vans had pulled up alongside, so Kim gathered that the decanting process was about to begin.

She followed the others down the steps again, listening to their excited chatter. A minute or so later, the tour guide hustled up and thrust a plastic-wrapped loaf of sliced bread into her hands. "Compliments of the management." He beamed and gestured toward the smaller vans. "Take your places, please. We'll get underway just as soon as everybody's aboard."

Kim felt a tap on her shoulder and a male voice saying, "Your transportation's here." She turned obediently, and then drew in her breath to see Gray standing there, his glance even sharper than usual.

Instinct made her take a step backward, holding out the loaf of bread like a shield. "No, thanks," he said laconically, "I ate on the ferry."

"It's not for eating—I mean for people," she began and then broke off when she caught his amused expression. She drew herself up to ask, "What in the dickens are you doing here?"

"Looking for my missing fiancée. What else? That reminds me, I'd better let that tour guide know that you're dropping out. He's giving us a dirty look."

"But I'm not dropping out," she countered, rallying to the cause. "I want to see this place."

"And so you shall. But I think it would be better if you did it with me." The steely undertone in his voice belied his polite proposal. So did his hand in the middle of her back as he directed her toward his car parked behind the vans. "Go get in—I'll tell the tour people you've made other plans."

Aside from pitching a screaming fit in the middle of the parking lot, which wouldn't endear her to the other passengers, Kim realized that she couldn't do much but comply. She watched Gray go over to the tour guide and then turned her back on the discussion to get in his car. Her annoyance was rapidly fading, and, aside from his high-handedness in planning the rest of her day, she was secretly delighted that he'd come on her trail. At least she hoped that concern was one reason for his prompt pursuit.

She wasn't so sure a few minutes later when he came back to the car and slid behind the steering wheel. "You're all set," he said, dropping another loaf of bread on the seat beside them. "I told him we got our signals mixed and that I'd been wanting to see this place for a long time. Since the tour gets out of buying your admission to the place, the fellow even tossed in an extra loaf of bread for goodwill." When Kim stared coolly back at him, he added, "I must say that he looked happier about the switch than you do."

"Most people prefer to be asked. Press gangs went out of style in the eighteenth century," she informed him. Then, afraid that she might be overdoing her reluctance and end up back on that miserable bus after all, she said, "I didn't think that you'd be back this soon."

He shrugged as he reached for the ignition key. "They sailed on schedule this morning and even gave us a free breakfast aboard to make up for the inconvenience. I'm glad that you left a note in the room so I knew where to look."

Was that why she'd left it? Kim wondered. Probably she'd been hoping subconsciously that he'd do exactly that. Certainly the day suddenly seemed brighter, and for the first time she felt as excited about the prospect of touring the Game Farm as all the rest of those people.

Gray started the car and backed out of the parking area, letting the tour vans precede him. "There's no rush," he said, surprising her with his relaxed air. "I'd just as soon not be in line. Take a look at this map. Is there more than one route through the farm? After we drive down and reach the main gate?"

"It seems like it. There are a couple of loop trails, so we can see which is the more deserted." She looked up from the brochure when he slowed a few minutes later and turned at the end of a high fence into a main gate for the farm. A pleasant young man in uniform leaned out from a ticket booth to collect their admission money and told them to take the roads at their leisure. He again cautioned them to stay in the car except for the walking tour area around the big cats' enclosure and the petting area to their left.

Gray thanked him and drove on, choosing the road to the right. He spared a glance for the petting section the guard had mentioned, where some pygmy goats, sheep, and several tortoises were the center of attention. "Just like a children's zoo," he commented.

"There are quite a few adults in there, too," Kim mentioned, craning to see over his shoulder.

"Is that a hint?" Gray was driving so slowly along the track that it was no trouble for him to give her a quizzical glance.

"It could be," she admitted. "The only thing against it is the mud." She gestured toward the soggy ground on either side of the car where animal tracks stood out clearly. "At least it isn't raining now. Will the overcast days make your brother postpone his filming here?"

Gray's stern mouth relaxed. "The last time I saw him he was checking weather tables and available witch doctors. That's one reason I'm here—I'm supposed to report on—"

"—how deep the mud is?" Kim tossed him a gamine grin. "It's all right—you don't have to be diplomatic. The natives have heard that kind of talk before."

"And do a great deal to spread the propaganda, I'll warrant." He gestured toward the scenic hills surrounding the Game Farm. The evergreen foliage was a striking panorama in varying shades and hues, with a capsule view down the valley toward the shimmering waters of the Strait. "You're just trying to keep all this for yourself."

"We do encourage a few selected tourists at Port Lathrop," she told him solemnly. "Oh, good heavens! Look who's coming to lunch!"

"Ready or not." Gray chuckled and braked to a stop as a dignified llama headed purposefully toward them. "Don't lower your window too far or you'll have her head in your lap," he cautioned as Kim excitedly tore open the plastic wrapping and extracted a crust of bread.

"I see what you mean. Grandma, what big teeth you have," she gulped and lowered the glass a discreet four inches.

"Take it easy or you'll come away short on fingers

next time," Gray told her when the bread disappeared in one fast movement.

"It's your turn now." Kim prudently rolled up her window an inch. "Look, she's coming around to you for a second helping."

"Obviously an old hand at free lunches." Gray managed to dispose of his bread without coming so close to disaster.

"She doesn't fit the 'crust of bread' role—see how she's looking down that long nose at you."

"As if she'd like to spit in my eye."

"Only camels do that—I think."

"Ummm. Well, I'm not taking any chances." Gray shifted gears and edged on down the track. "Besides, we've got to make our bread go around. There's a regiment of zebra up ahead."

"And all those bears over in the pasture."

"They get their slice thrown to them," Gray said definitely. "I'm not going nose to nose with one of those monsters."

"Or tooth to tooth?"

"Not even with a ten-foot pole. Want to feed a deer or go on to those zebras?"

"Let's do both." Her eyes were shining with excitement as she turned to him. "Oh, Gray, this is fun!"

The next hour went by faster than either of them could have believed. After completing the northern loop road, they parked and walked around the caged area with lions and Siberian tigers on one side and jaguars and leopards on the other. At the end of the row, powerful wolves watched from another group of wire cages, their thick silvery-gray coats rippling as the animals moved gracefully inside the well-kept enclosures.

"I think I like it better when I'm the one cooped up," Kim said as they made their way back to the car and got in.

"Ummm." Gray was solemnly counting the number of slices he had left from his loaf of bread. "Don't interrupt, this is important."

"You look like somebody fingering pieces of gold," she told him, amused by his concentration. "What's all that for?"

"We still have one more loop to go," he said, jerking his head toward a dirt track which circled to the south of the big-cat enclosure. "According to the brochure, that means deer, yak, donkeys, elk, and bison. We're getting low on the calories, so no more doubling up."

"I just weakened on that one zebra," she muttered, counting her own precious hoard. "We should have brought more bread."

"Next time we'll know better." Gray started the car but allowed two of the tour vans a good distance ahead before shifting into drive.

This time, the pastures were fenced with sturdy posts instead of electric current to keep some of the species apart, and there were cattle grids on the roads so that the big animals couldn't wander that way.

Despite her best intentions to allow one slice per animal, Kim was enchanted by a huge, shaggy yak with strong yellow teeth and a molting appearance. She allowed him to chomp onto her next-to-the-last slice of bread and then told Gray sheepishly, "He looks an awful lot like a moth-eaten moose head that hangs in the town library."

Gray kept his own window tightly shut to keep the

yak from his side of the car. "That's the third slice he's conned out of you. And no, I won't."

"What do you mean?"

"Share mine with you," he said solemnly. "It's no use going all wide-eyed. There are some donkeys down the road who are getting my last crust."

Kim turned to survey the big head still at her window. Only the rubber stamp of a nose could manage to penetrate the open part, but the yak was hanging tough. "Sorry, love," she told him. "You heard the man."

Gray chuckled and pulled away, accelerating carefully so that the big animal had ample time to stand back. "That lump hasn't missed a meal in years. He just knows a patsy when he sees one."

Despite his ultimatum, Gray insisted that Kim get his last two pieces of bread after they'd run the gamut of donkeys on his side of the road. "There's a bunch of bison mixed with some elk down there by the petting area," he said as they let the two vans put some distance ahead of them. "From the looks of things, the elk will get most of the largess from those tour buses—we can't let the bison think they've been left out in the cold."

"So I'm not the only softie," she told him, laughing.

"I just like the bison. Good Lord, they look big! Especially next to those pygmy goats."

"Like a skyscraper next to a log cabin," she agreed. "I'm surprised they let those little fellows in this enclosure. If one of those bison leaned the wrong way, he'd squash those poor goats!"

Gray nodded, braking by the group of a half-dozen formidable bison, who started ambling toward their car. "It looks to me as if the pygmies wandered out of the petting area by the entrance. Maybe some child left that gate open."

"We'd better report it when we go out. It's too bad somebody can't shoo them out of the way."

Gray looked at the solid phalanx of bison approaching and said softly, "No dice. Remember the first rule of the park—don't get out of your car!" He frowned as he stared through the windshield and then said tersely, "Open your window! Wave that bread around!"

"To get their attention? But there's such a little bit—"

"Do as I say," he cut in. "Damn, it *would* happen. . . ."

She followed his gaze to see that one of the vans ahead of them—in backing slightly to avoid a muddy pool on the track—had collided with one of the little goats, who'd collapsed in a heap by the rear tire.

"Gray! Do you see? That poor baby," she gasped incoherently. "And that other van—"

"—is backing in the same place." He reached for his door handle.

"They'll run over him, too! My God, what are you doing?"

"Keep those bison occupied on your side of the car," he flung over his shoulder as he set off at a dead run toward the fallen animal.

Frantically, Kim did as he asked and ran her window down so far that she almost had two entire bison heads in her lap before she regained her senses. She shoved the bread at them, still trying to see what was happening to Gray at the other side of the track. He was shouting and waving, but evidently the van driver couldn't hear him over the engine noise. Kim shut her eyes in horror rather than watch the rear end of the vehicle go over the injured goat again.

An instant later, she opened them to see Gray hurrying back to the car with the wounded animal clutched against his chest. She gasped as she saw some of the bison shuffle nervously, their nostrils flaring. One of the largest bulls, who had remained haughtily aloof from the feeding, started ominously toward Gray's approaching figure.

Kim slid across the seat and unlatched the door, swinging it wide just in time to allow Gray to detour and reach the car after avoiding the big bull. "Here! Take him!" he ordered Kim without ceremony as he slid onto the seat.

It wasn't easy, because there wasn't much room for the transfer of the goat under the steering wheel, but they managed, and Gray got his door closed just seconds before the bull and two of his friends came to call.

By that time, the poor little pygmy was quaking with fear, jerking frantically to escape, and it was all Kim could do to keep him on her lap.

"Broken leg," Gray said tersely. "And all this hasn't helped."

"It's better than being dead," Kim said, trying to soothe the creature.

"That's what I thought." Gray had started the car by then. "Hang on. We'll find somebody to look after him."

He drove back down the track, lurching onto the muddy soft shoulder around the two tourist vans parked so their occupants could feed a herd of guanaco. The car wheels spun in the mire at the last moment, and Kim held her breath until there was traction and they were up on the harder surface again. Gray accelerated through an empty pasture, not slowing until they finally drove past the petting area and pulled up as close as possible to the administration building just beyond. "You're okay?" he wanted to know, pausing with one leg halfway out of the car. "Can you hang onto him a little longer?"

"I'm okay," she confirmed, stroking the goat's head gently. "I just hope he is."

Gray nodded and took care not to slam the door as he closed it. "I'll be as quick as I can," he promised and loped toward the administration quarters.

Kim took her gaze from their patient just long enough to notice that they had the attention of most petting-area residents by then. A black-nosed sheep came a few steps toward the car and stared intently. Another pygmy goat—much like the one she held except for patches of mud on his knees—approached, stiff-legged, to see what was going on. Even the head of the big tortoise nearby moved toward the car like a slow pendulum, as if he'd scented possible danger.

The pale early-spring sunshine filtering through the gray cloud cover couldn't dispel the atmosphere of brooding tension. The solitary plump crow swooping overhead reminded Kim of a vulture waiting for his prey, and her clasp tightened instinctively on her helpless little captive.

Then, without warning, the scene exploded into action. Gray shoved open the door of the administration building and hurried back to the car, closely followed by two husky young men in the olive-green uniforms of the Game Farm. An attractive girl wearing the same kind of outfit wasn't far behind them, but she headed for a van with the Game Farm logo which was parked near the main gate.

"It's okay," Gray called to Kim as they approached. "They wanted to put in a call to the vet."

"He's just down the road and waiting for us," one of the wardens told Kim as they came up to the car and carefully opened the door beside her. "Well, old fellow," he said, laying a gentle hand on the pygmy's head, "now see what you've gone and done. Let me have the needle, Tom," he went on to the other man in a soft expressionless tone. "We'll make the trip easier for him."

He had slipped the hypodermic needle under the skin and given the shot almost before Kim knew what was happening. Then he handed the hypo back to the other warden and smiled reassuringly at their anxious faces. "All finished. Now Little Mac won't do any more damage to that leg on the way. Just hang on to him a minute longer until that shot takes effect."

"He will wake up, won't he?" Kim asked fearfully, seeing how quickly the little animal was surrendering to the drug.

"Lord, yes!" The fellow who'd administered the shot grinned at her. "This'll just give us a chance to put a rough splint on in the van. Moving doesn't help in a case like this." Seeing Kim open her mouth to explain, he held up a big palm. "In your case, I'm mightly glad you did. Little Mac's a pillar of this place." He leaned down to survey their patient and nodded in satisfaction. "We can move him now."

The man named Tom signaled for the girl driving the van to pull alongside and then went to open the rear door so the transfer could be made.

Kim and Gray watched like anxious parents until they saw Little Mac carefully placed on a mattress and the two wardens get in beside him.

"Come back and see him when he's receiving visitors. We'll make sure you get a blue-ribbon tour," the older man said as Gray helped close the doors.

Gray nodded and stepped back out of the way as the girl driving the van accelerated carefully from the muddy forecourt out onto the hard-surfaced highway. He shoved his hands in his pockets and stared after it until he heard a suspicious sniff at his side. "Hey, you're not crying," he said, rounding on Kim, who was searching through her purse.

"Certainly not. Blast it!" The last came when she didn't find what she was looking for.

"Here." Gray shoved a clean white handkerchief in her hand and said quietly, "He'll be fine. The vet is waiting in his surgery to take over. Apparently Little Mac is the pet of the whole farm. I learned that the town's school children donated the pygmy goats *and* named them. He'll probably have more visitors while he's recovering than those koalas in San Diego."

Kim realized that he was talking to give her a chance to pull herself back together after all the excitement. She managed a shaky smile and asked, "Does Little Mac have a brother?"

Gray grinned, reading her mind again. "Probably. What do you bet that he's bigger?"

"Then I won't ask what he's called." She shook her head, smiling as she thought about it. "Little Mac was so good through the whole thing."

"You were pretty good yourself. At least you rate a bang-up dinner for your efforts." Gray walked around to get behind the wheel. "I suppose we should go back and change clothes first."

"Heavens, yes." She smiled at him wryly. "Now I know what they mean by the expression 'smell like a goat.' But it was worth it."

Her last remark was so quiet that it barely carried to Gray's ears, but he paused before turning on the ignition. His smoke-colored eyes were warmer than usual, and there was a crooked smile softening his stern mouth. "Definitely worth it." The smile broadened to a grin as he shifted into drive and started toward the highway which went to Port Victor. "We'll have to celebrate his recovery with champagne, at least."

Kim smiled back at him and settled in her corner of the car with a wriggle of satisfaction. For a day that had started so bleakly, things were certainly looking up!

Chapter Seven

On the drive back to the resort, Gray only made sporadic attempts at idle conversation to break the silence in the car. There was a natural letdown after all the excitement at the Game Farm, and he seemed to recognize it. He asked casually if Kim wanted the heater on and a little later commented on a sailboat flotilla racing for a buoy in the Strait. Aside from that, he kept his attention on the winding two-lane road with only occasional glances toward the lush green overgrowth around them.

Kim settled back in the cocoon of warm air which surrounded them, wondering how such a prosaic thing as a rented car could become a secluded haven. She liked the way Gray was treating her just then—not a solicitous "poor little woman" attitude nor "let's pretend that nothing happened," which would have been even worse. He was relaxed and had a strangely content expression—as if highly satisfied with the way things had gone.

She rested her head against the corner of the leather seat and uttered a soft sigh as she thought about it. Gray must have heard, because he shot her an inquisitive glance, which softened as he encountered her dreamy gaze. Then, just as abruptly, he turned his attention to the road again without commenting.

When they reached the resort, he pulled into a parking spot as close to their room as he could manage and said, "How long will it take you to get ready?"

"Half an hour—if that's all right."

His lips quirked as if he found her anxious tone amusing. "Take your time. I didn't mean that we had to hurry. I'll go check at the front desk and see if there are any messages and make our dinner reservation. That way, you can have first crack at the shower and I'll stay out from underfoot."

Kim was about to give him full marks for tact when another thought occurred to her. She paused, halfway out of the car. "How could there be any messages—real ones, I mean—when nobody knows that we're here?" Then she remembered something she'd tried to forget. "Except for Carola, of course."

"She just knows we're somewhere in Port Victor, unless Scott gave her any more information. I called him last night from Canada." Gray kept his voice casual as he got out of his side of the car and dropped the ignition key in his pocket.

"I see." She made her own tone match his. "Was it difficult to tell him about all this?"

Gray's shoulders shook with sudden laughter. "The hardest part was explaining why you couldn't come to the phone so he could give you his best wishes."

Mischief was in her own glance as she surveyed him across the top of the car. "Do I dare ask why I couldn't make it?"

"As I recall, you were taking a nap. To make up

for the sleep we'd lost the night before. He didn't pursue the topic."

"I'll do as much for you sometime," she replied dryly. "Is there anything else I should know?"

"Just that he expects to get a cut rate for his crew at the Stratford now that it's in the family." Gray slammed his car door and stood there with his hands in his pockets. "I told him that you had my permission to charge double."

"Then he doesn't know that we aren't—that we haven't—"

"Tied the knot?" Gray's expression settled in its more familiar austere lines. "Hell, no! That's one story that isn't about to change. Besides"—he shot a glance at the watch on his wrist—"in six and a half hours, more or less, the waiting period will be over and we can make it a *fait accompli.*"

"You mean with a justice of the peace at midnight?" she asked, wide-eyed.

"Well, that's one way of solving the problem. You'd better get changed."

"All right." She noticed that he didn't waste any time striding up through the parking area toward the administration section of the resort as she thought about his last comment. Matrimony wasn't a way to solve any problem, but she supposed it could be rationalized as a stopgap measure in their case. Gray had been careful not to mention a time period before they set about getting an annulment afterward. Probably he'd spent his day in Canada giving thanks that an annulment was still possible—that they hadn't changed the rules to include a weekend affair.

Besides, Kim thought bitterly as she walked down the hall and unlocked the door to their room, that sort of thing would just be exchanging one hurt for another. No matter how much publicity there was on "modern" life-styles, emotions didn't always work in tandem with common sense. Gray might be able to walk away unscathed from a brief torrid involvement, but she knew that she'd be miserable.

Her lips twisted derisively as she saw the package containing her attractive blue nightgown and negligee in her suitcase as she went in the dressing room. Talk about flying in the face of fate! At least there'd only be one more night that she'd be stuck with the cotton pajamas, she told herself. As soon as she got back to the Stratford, she'd drive a stake through the accursed things.

A hot shower made her feel better, and she told herself that dinner would complete the transformation. When she finished in the bathroom, she made sure that the mat was neatly placed back on the tub and that plenty of clean towels remained stacked on the chrome rack. After all, there was no use giving Gray the wrong idea of living together even before they'd made it legal.

She heard his key in the lock when she'd finished dressing and was in front of the mirror applying her lipstick. Apparently he approved of her coffee-colored silk broadcloth coatdress with its slim skirt and flattering nipped-in waistline, because his eyebrows lifted and he let out a soundless whistle.

"Quite a transformation." He pocketed the key. "Looks as if I timed this about right."

"The bath's all yours," she assured him with a final look at her reflection in the mirror. "I'll go read a book or watch television or something while you're getting ready."

"I thought you'd suggest something like that," he said, coming into the dressing room and taking off his jacket. "You do credit to that Victorian environment of yours. What would happen if I suggested that you make yourself useful?"

She frowned. "In what way?"

"Such a suspicious woman," he said, reaching for a hanger. "For openers, you could scrub my back."

Kim met his taunting glance. "You should have mentioned it earlier and then I wouldn't have bothered to get dressed. This fabric spots so dreadfully," she added, smoothing her silk skirt against her thigh.

"Touché." He reached up and traced a star against the steamy glass. "One up to you. I won't be long—our dinner reservation's in forty minutes."

Kim didn't bother to hide her smile as she nodded. "Right. I'll see what's on the tube. I haven't heard any news for a day or so—maybe the world's come to an end and they forgot to tell us."

She strolled out of the dressing room, trying to give the impression that the television schedule was the only thing which interested her just then. Certainly not the fleeting glimpse of Gray's broad shoulders when he tossed his shirt in the direction of his suitcase or the way he moved when he headed in to turn on the bathwater.

And if she kept up that kind of thinking, she told herself bitterly, she'd need to stick her head in the ice bucket to come back to her senses.

Fortunately, the television newscast focused on all the world-wide horrors that had occurred in the last twenty-four hours, so she was able to ignore her own personal disaster, who was whistling happily just thirty feet away. She kept her eyes glued on the set when the bathroom door finally opened and she heard him come into the dressing room.

Evidently he was listening to the news program, too, because when he emerged in a dark-gray suit worn with a paler-gray shirt and burgandy-striped tie he said, "It's a good thing I allowed time for a drink before dinner."

She turned off the television with relief. "I don't think I need one tonight. There was just one Mideast terrorist attack and a partial revolution in South America."

Gray reached for his room key on the bureau. "You mean it hasn't spoiled your appetite?"

"Nope. I'm starving," she said lightly, picking up her purse. "Let's eat fast before there's a worldwide famine."

"Or the electricity goes out in Port Victor." He opened the door, ushering her ahead of him into the corridor. "My sentiments exactly."

Kim was intrigued when he led her around the front of the resort and into a Japanese restaurant near the city pier. "This is new, isn't it?" she asked, glancing with pleasure at the shadowed interior with its painted beamed ceiling. The tables were separated by artfully placed potted plants to create an air of intimate dining, and the waitresses were kimono-garbed orientals who whisked around efficiently.

Gray gave their name to a hovering maître d', who checked his reservation list and then beckoned for them to follow. "Somebody told me this place is good," Gray said in a low voice. "It's not all sushi bar or raw vegetables either. I checked the menu earlier."

They were seated at a round table with a tiled top and handed the bill of fare with instructions to enjoy their dinner. Kim settled back in her leather-covered chair with a smile, glad that the low hum of conversation from the other diners wasn't loud enough to be distracting. Light from a wrought-iron chandelier and the hurricane lantern on their table made it possible to read the print on the menu but very little more. "If I spill anything on my tie, I'll never know until later," Gray observed, tipping his menu toward the flickering candlelight. "It's a good thing that this type is big. What sounds good to you—prawns, steak, or chicken?"

Kim caught an appetizing whiff as a waitress passed with some dishes en route to a neighboring table. "Everything," she murmured. "Maybe a little of each."

"Want to start with the sushi bar?"

She shook her head regretfully. "I'm not hungry enough for raw fish, but I'll settle for practically anything else."

"You don't have to apologize," Gray said, sounding amused. "We can experiment another night."

Kim murmured absently and watched as he gave their order to the waitress, who materialized with glasses of ice water and cups for their green tea. From the calm way that Gray had mentioned "another night," it sounded as if he didn't plan to leave the area immediately after getting married. Probably he'd stay long enough in Port Lathrop to stop any tongues wagging and then fly south under the pretext of business. Which was all she could hope for, Kim told herself severely, and then looked up, startled, when Gray's voice penetrated. "I beg your pardon," she said, surprised to find that they were alone again.

"I just wondered what was wrong," he said. "You looked as if you'd seen a ghost for a minute there.

How about some tea?" The last came when a smiling busboy dressed in a black coolie coat added hot water to a big teapot on the table between them.

"Yes, thanks." She took a deep breath, deciding to enjoy the present and stop worrying about what the future held. "That busboy is the only one out of character in here—he's wearing jeans with that coat."

"Well, don't look in the kitchen or you might be even more disillusioned. The last time I ate in a Mexican restaurant, I noticed that the chef had sent out for Chinese food and seemed to be thoroughly enjoying it. Umm—this looks good."

His last comment came when a smiling Japanese girl deposited plates of crisp green salad in front of them. Gray hefted the pair of chopsticks that were beside his silverware and gave Kim a quizzical look.

"No way," she told him politely but firmly and picked up her fork.

After that, there was a satisfied silence while they finished their salad to the last morsel. They sat back then, watching a chef wheel a grill in front of them to prepare the rest of their dinner. Without a wasted motion, he chopped and sautéed a plateful of shrimp, finally adding long slivers of zucchini and onion to be heated through.

That course was skillfully transferred to warmed plates, and he motioned for them to enjoy it while he prepared lean New York steaks. These were sliced into small squares and cooked on the grill with a wonderfully fragrant mixture of butter and spices. In the middle of the meat preparation, the cook dumped a heaping platter of fresh mushrooms and bean sprouts alongside to be fried gently. Then, when all of the food had reached the right degree of doneness, he motioned to another waitress, who quickly brought bowls of rice to the table together with side dishes of mustard and a soy-sauce mixture.

At that moment, the chef whisked away the remains of the prawn course and set the steaming meat platters in front of them. He smiled and bowed before quickly wheeling the grill away.

Kim speared a bite of steak and chewed it. "It's so tender!" she enthused to Gray, who was dipping some rice into the soy sauce. "You're a genius to have found this place."

"At least it's a step in the right direction. You haven't had many things to enjoy for the past day or so." He kept his glance carefully on his dinner as he added, "I'm sorry about leaving you stranded last night. A broken-down ferry never entered my calculations."

"You couldn't know." Kim kept her tone carefully bland, enjoying their dinner too much to risk open warfare again. She took another bite of steak before saying, "Did you try phoning your brother again tonight?"

"Yes, but he was out. It doesn't matter—if there's an emergency, he can call us here. I told him earlier that we wanted some privacy this weekend. Tomorrow, I'll have to let my company know where I can be reached. Since they pay me a salary," he said with a crooked grin, "they're inclined to be hardheaded about such things. More tea?"

"Yes, please." Kim felt a surge of relief that the beauteous Carola wasn't going to knock on their door after all. At least not until they reappeared at the Stratford.

They finished dinner with a rainbow sherbet, which

didn't follow the oriental theme but tasted wonderfully cool nonetheless. After that, to Kim's surprise, Gray mentioned a movie in town that he'd been wanting to see for some time and suggested they could still make the late showing. She tried to hide her surprise that he'd opt for such a diversion just then. Probably he thought it best to postpone returning to their room for as long as possible, she thought with wry amusement. The least she could do was agree and show some enthusiasm for the idea.

Before the silence could lengthen, she assured him fervently that she'd been wanting to see that movie because of its wonderful reviews. She didn't tell him that she'd seen it two weeks before in a preview and thought it was overrated. Noting his obvious relief, she decided that she'd managed to do something else right. By the time the movie was over, she'd be so sleepy that sharing a room again shouldn't pose any problems at all.

The movie hadn't changed in the interim and Gray's reaction to the plot paralleled hers, so she was pleasantly relaxed when they walked back to get in the car afterward. Her easygoing mood shattered like crystal when Gray looked at his watch after unlocking the car door and remarked, "Right on schedule, as advertised."

She stared up at him in the faint illumination of one of Port Victor's turn-of-the-century streetlights. "I beg your pardon?"

"I said, we're right on schedule."

"Schedule for what?"

He nudged her onto the front seat and closed the door behind her, finally going around to get in his side of the car before answering. "The waiting period.

Our waiting period. Ten more minutes and we can get this thing over with."

She winced at the decisive way he bit off the words and felt compelled to match his tone. "I don't see what that has to do with anything. They may have twenty-four-hour chapels in Las Vegas, but not . . ." She broke off, wide-eyed, as he shook his head. "You don't mean that you've arranged something for tonight?"

Gray inserted the ignition key with his usual economy of movement and started the car. "It wasn't difficult. Mr. Perkins thought it was heartening in this day and age that two people couldn't wait to tie the knot."

"Mr. Perkins?" she asked faintly, only vaguely aware that he'd made a U-turn on the deserted street and was heading for the hill which loomed over the business section of Port Victor.

"Justice of the peace," Gray explained. He didn't slacken his speed until he turned off the arterial a little later onto a tree-lined residential street which ran atop the bluff. "This way, it'll all be legal." He uttered a noise that was somewhere between a snort and a stifled laugh. "Damned if I ever thought that I'd feel guilty, but it seems to me I've been looking over my shoulder ever since we got here."

"Umm. I know what you mean," Kim murmured. It was reassuring that Gray didn't make a habit of clandestine weekends, although it was obvious he was well acquainted with the feminine sex. Even one kiss had shown that he knew all the rules of the mating game and some of the finer points that she'd only dreamed about.

At that moment, Gray slowed to a stop in front of

a big Victorian house on the right-hand side of the street where a porch light still burned. As she waited for him to come around to her side of the car, Kim wondered about asking what plans he'd made for the rest of the night and then decided against it. It was going to take all her courage to stand up in front of a justice of the peace without having an argument en route to the front porch.

Kim looked around after he'd rung the old-fashioned bell by the door. "You're sure there's someone alive in here? I almost expect to see bats swooping down from the roof."

"I hear somebody coming now. If it's a ghost, it's an overweight one—" His voice stopped as the door creaked open and a balding man in his shirtsleeves peered out at them. "Mr. Perkins? I'm Gray Stanton and this is my fiancée, Miss Cosgrove."

"Of course, of course." A broad smile creased the older man's lined face. "Come in, both of you. We've been waiting up. I have to confess dozing off a couple of times. Right in here—I usually use the parlor for my ceremonies."

After that, everything moved so quickly that Kim could scarcely believe it was happening. Two gray-haired women arrived from another part of the house and stood automatically on one side of a littered desk. "Witnesses," Mr. Perkins announced in the tone of a man who'd said it many times before. Then Kim found herself lined up in front of the desk beside Gray, listening to Mr. Perkins's slightly querulous voice as he went rapidly through the ceremony. She had to swallow before she could manage to say "I do" in the proper place and noted thankfully that Gray's response was much firmer. When it came time for the ring, he slid a wide gold band on her finger without any fumbling, and when they were pronounced man and wife, Gray kissed her tremulous lips just long enough for both witnesses to utter an audible sigh of pleasure. Then Kim was shown where to sign the marriage certificate, and after Gray put his signature below hers, she was instructed to tuck the document in her purse. Kim found herself shaking hands and thanking the witnesses while Gray attended to the financial dealings with the now-beaming Mr. Perkins.

Before she knew it, they were ushered out onto the porch again and the door was shut behind them. In the parlor, the overhead light was extinguished, and an instant later the porch light went out, too.

"That's called speeding us on our way," Gray said, sounding amused as they descended the sagging wooden steps. "At least they're honest about wanting to get to bed."

Kim wasn't sure exactly what he meant by that remark and didn't dare ask just then. The whole scene was still so unreal that she almost pinched herself to make sure that she wasn't dreaming as he unlocked the car door and she got inside. She *did* lean forward to examine her ring in the dim dashboard light when he started the car and pulled out onto the street.

"If you don't like it, we can find something else," Gray said, with a sideways glance. "Probably I should have let you pick it out."

"It's beautiful," Kim said truthfully, admiring the ring's modern swirl design with its three colors of gold. She discovered suddenly that she was looking at the band through brimming eyes and had to fumble in her purse for a handkerchief to mop her damp cheeks.

The car slowed as Gray noticed her dilemma. "I'm sorry about all that," he said, sounding less assured than usual. "I hadn't realized the ceremony would be quite so cut-and-dried. Those two witnesses looked as if they'd been preserved in formaldehyde for the occasion."

Kim mopped her eyes and managed to smile. "Actually they were very nice and they thought the whole thing was terribly romantic. That we couldn't wait until morning, I mean." She looked down at her ring again as if fascinated to find it on her finger. "I couldn't disillusion them."

"Well, if you're not crying about that—what's the problem?"

"Women always cry at weddings."

"Not their own," Gray told her in the tone of a man who knew all about such things.

Kim's chin came up. "I do. And it's a free country." She sat up straighter and peered through the windshield, trying to see where they were going. "Is this the way back to the resort?"

"That's right. Why? Did you want to go somewhere else?"

"No, of course not. I just thought that maybe you'd made other plans."

"That marriage certificate is as far as I went," he said, slowing down to turn toward the shore from the business district. "Now that we're virtuous and unsullied, I intend to enjoy what's left of the night."

"I see." Kim tried to sound confident as she responded, but it was an effort. If Gray insisted on making enigmatic remarks like that and she kept imagining hidden meanings, she'd be a nervous wreck before morning.

Gray went on, saying calmly, "Tomorrow, we might call at the Game Farm and see if our patient is receiving visitors."

"You'll have to ask them what kind of an offering we should bring," Kim replied, happy for the change of subject. "Maybe Little Mac would like a bouquet of carrots."

"Or a collar of tin cans? Possibly an assortment so he could take his choice." Gray slowed to turn in the resort parking lot. "We must be the only people still wandering around—from the look of things, Port Victor's rolled up the sidewalks until morning."

His last remark came as he eased the car through the crowded but darkened parking area, trying to find an empty slot close to their room. The only illumination of the area came from a few strategically placed spotlights and a neon arrow which pointed toward the resort office.

Gray finally edged into a vacant spot near the big double glass doors of their wing and turned off the key. He sighed as he turned to face her. "It's been a long day. Do you have anything more in the trunk?"

"No, thanks." For an instant Kim wondered what happened if a bridegroom had to carry a heavy suitcase *and* his bride over the threshold. The fleeting vision made her giggle, but fortunately Gray was out of the car by then and coming around to open her door.

As they walked down the deserted corridor of the resort a minute or so later, the only noise came from ice cubes dropping in the complicated machine nearby. Gray pulled out his key as they approached the room, and Kim drew in her breath nervously. She wasn't sure whether she wanted him to make the pretense of swinging her over the threshold or simply ignore the whole thing.

When he followed the latter course and motioned her silently ahead of him into the room, she was surprised to feel a pang of dismay. Not that she should have expected anything else, she told herself fiercely. Despite that soulless marriage ceremony, Gray hadn't acknowledged the slightest change in their relationship. But then what had she expected? she thought dismally as she stood in the middle of their room and watched him close the door.

"I think we've earned some champagne," Gray announced, shedding his coat over the back of a chair as he came into the room. "It won't take long to call room service—hello, what's this?"

"What do you mean?" she asked as he stood poised over the telephone.

"The red light is blinking," he said, reaching for the receiver. "Generally that means a message. Probably the operator just made a mistake this time."

"Your brother knows we're here," she pointed out as he waited for the switchboard to answer.

"He wouldn't have called unless it was an emergency—" Gray broke off when the operator answered and then waited again as she hunted for the message. When it was delivered, he said, "Yes, I'd appreciate it if you'd get the number for me."

"What's going on?" Kim whispered as he stood waiting. "Is there anything wrong with your brother?"

Gray put his hands over the mouthpiece and said tersely, "It isn't Scott—it's Carola."

"I thought she didn't know this number."

"I said I didn't give it to her," Gray replied impatiently. "There's a difference—" He waved her quiet as he spoke into the receiver again. "Hello—I want to speak to Miss Kenyon, please. Yes, I know what time it is, but this is urgent." He grimaced at Kim. "Apparently I've been put on the hold button. That's all I needed at this point."

"You're obviously not calling the Stratford," Kim deduced aloud. "We've never had a hold button in the place. Carola must have checked out to stay somewhere else. Do you suppose she got into a fight with Ozzie? He can be pretty hardheaded at times."

"Carola isn't the kind of woman who'd fight with a caretaker. She'd forget he was there most of the time and ignore him the rest."

"Then maybe she just wanted to give you her new address," Kim said with deceptive mildness. "In case you wanted to get in touch."

"Keep up with that attitude and I'll get in closer touch with you than you'd prefer, Madame Stanton," Gray warned. "Carola and I don't have that kind of relationship. She's merely a prospective sister-in-law as far as I'm concerned. Besides, I don't seem to be having much luck conducting any kind of affair these days. It's a pity I didn't call for that champagne earlier—" He broke off to say, "Hello—is that you, Carola? What in the devil's going on?" Then, a moment later, "I'm sorry that I snapped at you, but for pete's sake—stop crying!"

"Crying?" Kim murmured, feeling a twinge of alarm for the first time. No matter how disappointed Carola was with the state of things, she wouldn't be calling in the middle of the night to weep over the phone.

An instant later, it was confirmed when Gray said,

"Hit on the head! For God's sake, when did that happen?"

Kim hurried to his side, motioning for Gray to hold the receiver away from his ear so that she could hear, too. He nodded absently, sinking onto the side of the bed and pulling her down beside him with his free hand. "Carola—slow down—I can't understand you when you talk so fast."

"Is she badly hurt?" Kim asked, trying to catch up.

Gray waved a hand to shush her and said impatiently in the telephone, "Then there's nobody at the inn? Is that right?" A spate of excited explanations came through the receiver, and Gray's eyebrows went up as he gave Kim a speaking look. He made no attempt to stem the barrage until Carola evidently took time to breathe. "I understand," he soothed. "I hope that you told Scott you were okay. All we need now is to have him fly north and join the party." He rubbed the back of his neck wearily as he listened to Carola again. Kim felt a sudden urge to pull his head down on her shoulder and comfort him. She abandoned such fantasy in a hurry when he said, "I'm glad you let us know, honey," suddenly aware that he was talking to Carola again and not to his new wife. "We'll leave right away and be there as soon as we can. Right. We'll see you in the morning."

He hung up then and turned to survey Kim, his expression not giving anything away.

"I gather," she said carefully, "that Carola's going to have a night's sleep, but that we're not."

"You could say that." He surveyed her wryly. "This has turned out to be one hell of a weekend."

"It wasn't what I planned either," Kim pointed out.

"I'm not talking about getting married—"

"And I'm sorry if Carola got into trouble," Kim went on, ignoring his interruption, "but it can't be too serious. Not if she had enough strength to carry on over the phone the way she did."

"She didn't get hurt at all. Just scared out of her socks. Ozzie was the victim." Gray's mouth settled in an ominous line as he reported, "Your watchman is in the hospital with multiple head injuries."

"Ozzie!" Kim swallowed and tried again. "What happened, for heaven's sake?"

"Apparently he caught somebody trying to break in earlier tonight and got hit over the head—hard. He'll recover, but it'll be a while." Gray went on reflectively, "At the moment the police are wondering exactly what you've got at the inn that's worth all the commotion."

Chapter Eight

"If they're serious, they can certainly take a look at the inventory," Kim said, wide-eyed as she stared back at him. "The only valuable things are some of the big pieces of furniture, and they'd have to be taken out with a crane—I know, because that's the way we got one of them in. And they're not hidden—there are tours of the inn every afternoon in season or any other time if some Victoriana buff comes calling." She rubbed her forehead with her fingertips as she tried to think. "It doesn't make sense. Poor Ozzie. Are they sure he'll be all right?"

"The hospital reports he's in stable condition, but they want to keep him for observation to be on the safe side. Carola refused to stay in the inn afterwards—in case whoever it was came back. She locked the door and headed for a hotel downtown."

Kim nodded as she got to her feet. "I can't blame her. What an awful thing!"

"Apparently she woke up with all the commotion and went downstairs to find Ozzie collapsed by the open front door." Gray stood up and looked around the room. "I'd better see about checking out of here. Will it take you long to pack?"

She shook her head. "Ten minutes or so. Shall I meet you at the car?"

"No, never mind. We'll both pack and check out last thing."

"But you can't feel up to driving back to Port Lathrop tonight either," she said, sounding more woeful than she intended.

He reached over and smoothed her cheek with the back of his fingers. "It wasn't on my schedule, but you won't rest easy, knowing that the Stratford is without a night watchman."

"Especially after an attack on Ozzie," she said casually not wanting him to know that she was still feeling his touch even after he'd dropped his hand.

"Then start packing," Gray told her. "I'll call the police department at Port Lathrop and see if they can keep an eye on the place until we get there and make other plans."

"That would help. I'm sorry that you've been lumbered with all this. Nothing has turned out the way it should have all weekend."

He took her by the shoulders and moved her in the direction of the dressing room. "We can discuss that another time. Now, take off that pretty dress and change into something fit for sleeping in the car. There's no point in your staying awake all the way to Port Lathrop. Need any help with your bags?"

"Not really." Kim decided that she'd better get with it and bury her new satin nightgown and negligee in the suitcase before Gray started wondering when—or still more important, why—she'd bought them.

"I'll call the police in the meantime and stay out of your way," he said, sitting back down on the edge of his bed and reaching for the telephone. "Shall I tell them you'll be in touch in the morning?"

"Of course." She gestured with open palms. "Not that I'll be much help."

"No undiscovered Tiffany lamps or Fabergé eggs in the attic?"

"Only dust and spiders," she told him from the dressing room. "The fire department doesn't like anything stored up there or anyplace else."

"Well, keep thinking."

It was easy for him to say, Kim thought with wry amusement as she heard the murmur of his voice placing the long-distance call while she gathered up slacks and a sweater to change into. A glimpse of the full ice bucket reminded her of the champagne celebration that had gone aglimmering with the phone call. Now even that gesture of civility was abandoned. Once they returned to the Stratford, Gray could go back to his basement room and she'd be safely up on the second floor.

"Damn it to hell!" she said, after dropping her hairbrush with a clatter into the empty bathtub.

"Anything wrong?" Gray asked a moment later, catching her bending inelegantly to pick it up.

"Not a thing." Kim tried to sound offhand as she reached for a sweater to pull on over her lacy camisole. "Did you get your call through?"

"Uh-huh." He didn't miss her determinedly casual air and flushed cheeks. "I'd offer to help," he went on as she struggled to pull it over her head, "except that the house detective or some long-lost boyfriend of yours would materialize at the door if I put a finger on you."

"At least this doesn't have a zipper," she told him,

finally settling the sweater into place. "Besides, everything's legal now."

"So it is. I keep forgetting."

"That's either the sign of a troubled conscience . . ."

"Or a clear one," he said, pulling a shirt off the hanger. "Finished in the bathroom?"

She grabbed up her comb and nodded. "Finished period. Except for closing my bags."

It wasn't long before Gray had changed into slacks and a jacket for the drive back to Port Lathrop and carried their things to the car. Kim waited for him while he detoured by the resort office to pay the bill. For an instant she thought of offering to share the cost of the room but thought better of it when she glimpsed his determined profile. It wasn't the time to start another argument, she reasoned, and then smiled to herself, knowing that she wouldn't have exhibited such diplomacy earlier.

She did offer to drive on the return trip—an offer which was courteously but firmly turned down. There wasn't any extraneous conversation as they sped through the darkness in the middle of the night. Gray drove rapidly but carefully, slowing for the winding stretches of the road and when they encountered an occasional milk truck or camper, but hovering on the speed limit the rest of the time. Kim stared through the windshield at the yellow divider line on the highway for about a half hour and then found it was an effort to keep her eyelids open.

She woke to a gentle hand on her thigh and Gray saying, "You'd better sit up—we're almost at the Stratford."

She yawned and then moved hastily aside, saying,

"I didn't mean to use you for a resting post. Why didn't you push me off, for heaven's sake?"

"I didn't dare," he countered solemnly. " 'Shoulders and the use thereof' are assets listed in that marriage certificate. You didn't read the fine print."

Kim put her palms on her hot cheeks to cool them, wishing that just once she could find something clever to say instead of staring stupidly back at him.

"Besides, you looked about six years old," Gray said, reading her mind again. "Maybe I should have checked your birth certificate more closely."

Kim knew that he was just trying to be kind again. Probably he'd seen her apprehensive look at the Stratford, whose silhouette looked ominous in a darkness relieved only by one dim streetlight. She heard Gray's sigh after he turned off the ignition, showing he wasn't anxious to enter the front door either. "Do you have a key?" he asked finally.

She nodded and reached for her purse. "We'd better call the hospital first thing and find out how Ozzie is."

"Right after we check out things here." He appropriated the door key and got out of the car. Wordlessly, he took a suitcase from her when she reached into the back to get it and then said, "I'll get the rest of the stuff later. What do you know—company already?"

She glanced over her shoulder, startled, and then relaxed as she saw the blue lights of a city police car coming up the block. When it slowed and braked beside their parked sedan, Gray said, "I'll find out if there's any late news and tell them you're back. Okay?"

"Yes, please." Kim was so tired that it was hard to get the words out properly. "I'll wait on the porch for you."

Which was silly, she told herself as she trudged up the walk. She should have gone inside—except that Gray had kept the door key, so she had an excuse not to enter the dark foyer alone. Instead, she sat down on the top porch step, leaning back against the pillar while she waited for the discussion down by the police car to end.

She must have closed her eyes again, because the next thing she knew Gray was shaking her shoulder and saying, "C'mon, wake up. This is no place to spend the rest of the night."

"Oh, Lord—I feel like Rip Van Winkle." She almost staggered in getting to her feet and then focused enough to see that the police car had driven away. "Is everything all right?"

"That depends." Gray kept a firm grip around her shoulders as they walked to the front door and he inserted the key. "It's been quiet around here, but Ozzie still isn't in any condition to identify who hit him. According to those two, nobody's sure whether he sustained the injury after being shoved down the stairs or whether it was in a struggle by the front door." As he spoke, he opened the thick wooden door and fumbled for the electric switch beside it.

Kim stayed leaning against the doorjamb as she watched Gray walk over and right the wooden chair lying on its side by the registration table. Then her glance discovered a dark stain on the wide-planked floor, and her stomach muscles tightened. To think of poor Ozzie lying there!

"Would you rather go down and stay at the hotel with Carola?" Gray asked brusquely. "It might be a better idea. I can sleep here for the rest of the night, and tomorrow you can arrange for a security guard."

Kim shook her head, wide awake again. "I'm all right. Besides, the Stratford is my responsibility—you're the one who should have a chance to walk away. And don't say anything about this being part of that marriage certificate."

"We won't argue about it," Gray said tersely. "Just go in there and sit down." He jerked his head toward the living room. "Stay there until I go through the rest of the house."

If Gray were determined to be dragged into this latest mess, she could try not to act like a frail vapid female. "I thought it was only women who looked under beds," she told him, trying to keep up her end of the bargain.

He pretended to consider her remark. "I'll admit that men generally are more interested in what's on top of the mattress. This time, though, it's different."

"Well, if you're going to nose around, at least take a poker," Kim said, walking over to the fireplace and handing him a heavy brass one.

"Oh, for Lord's sake . . ."

"I mean it. Otherwise, I'm coming with you."

"I'll be damned if you are." He saw her lips tremble before she could steady them and said roughly, "Oh, all right. Give me that thing."

"I promise to wait right here," Kim said, meekly sitting on the settee.

He glared at her, as if he'd like to say more, but turned away instead, muttering something unprintable.

His anger had apparently subsided when he came out of the kitchen a minute or so later and turned to inspect an unused parlor at the back of the inn. "Nothing there," he reported coming back. "One of the windows has been leaking."

Kim leaned back against the hard wood of the settee. "That's all we needed."

"It didn't leak much." He headed for the winding stairway. "I'll see what's going on upstairs."

This time it was longer before he reappeared, but there was a satisfied look on his face when he came down again and deposited the poker by the fireplace. "All clear. You'd better get to bed—there's still a little time before daylight." He went over to slide the bolt on the front door, saying over his shoulder, "I still have to get the bags out of the car. I'll bring yours up."

When he returned, he looked surprised to find her holding the door open for him. "I thought you were tired," he said, putting down two suitcases and a zipper suit bag on a bench beside her. "Don't worry. I won't forget to lock up," he added, turning to fix the bolt. "Now then—lead on and I'll carry your bags."

Kim took a deep breath and said defiantly, "I'm not going to sleep up in that bedroom."

He shot a puzzled glance toward the empty stairway and then surveyed her determined figure. "Why not? I went over the whole place. There's not a thing stirring—not even the family ghost."

Kim's fists tightened until she could feel her nails cutting into her palms. "I know I'm being silly, but I can't help it. I'm not going up there by myself tonight. Where are you going to sleep?" She uttered a sound that was half sob and half laughter then. "And please don't say 'on a plane going south' or I'll—I'll—" Her shoulders sagged as she admitted, "I don't know what I'd do."

"Don't be an idiot," Gray said, putting down her

suitcase again and pulling her against his shoulder.

"I'm sorry." She nuzzled under his jacket like a kitten seeking warmth and security. "I don't know what's the matter with me."

"I do." Gray smoothed the back of her head lightly as he bent over her. "You're exhausted—and it's not surprising. Let's go back down to the basement."

She managed a small chuckle from where she was still buried in his chest. "Inns don't have basements— not if people sleep in them. It's a lower level or garden section."

"You can show me the advertising brochure to-morrow," he said, pulling her head back by catching a thick strand of hair so he could survey her face. "That's better. You've some color in your cheeks again. For a minute, I thought I was going to have to lay you out on that settee and burn feathers or some-thing under your nose. Wasn't that what happened when Victorians swooned in the parlor?" He put her gently from him, picking up the suitcase again before saying, "Thank God we don't have to worry about candles tonight."

Kim obediently led the way, managing to turn off the lights behind them in the process and staying scrupulously out of Gray's way on the back stairs. "This is awfully nice of you," she said hesitantly once they'd reached the lower level and were in the familiar corridor. She pulled up in front of the first bedroom door—where everything had started in what seemed a lifetime ago. "I don't know how to thank you."

"For pete's sake, stop being grateful and open the door." Gray walked past her into the room to deposit both bags on the carpet and then swung the big one onto a luggage rack against the wall. "The next thing is to get you in bed before you fall on your face," he added in a conversational tone, opening her suitcase to rummage inside. "Where are those faded purple pajamas of yours?"

Kim had gone over to sit on the edge of the mattress, since she didn't seem able to stand up any longer. She frowned at his intent figure, determined to get one thing straight. "They're mauve."

He didn't look up from his task. "They're what?"

"My pajamas. They're mauve—not purple."

"Tonight I don't care if they're sky-blue with pink polka dots—" He broke off to whistle softly, and she saw that he had found her new purchases, lifting the lacy blue negligee to admire it.

"I could wear that," she offered, getting up her courage suddenly.

He shook his head and dropped the confection back in the suitcase. "No sense in wasting it," he said matter-of-factly, without the slightest tinge of regret. Suddenly he unearthed what he was looking for. "These pajamas will do the trick," he assured her, putting them on the bed beside her. "Can you manage to get into them?"

He might have been asking about an extra blanket—or a second helping of potatoes, Kim thought, and she straightened rebelliously. She *was* his wife, but if he were determined to ignore the fact, she could follow his lead. "Of course I can manage," she assured him. "I was just waiting until you left."

His eyes narrowed at her sudden hostility. "I've seen you peeled down a layer or two before this," he said without moving. "Right now, you don't look as if you could even pull that sweater over your head."

"Then I'll spend the rest of the night in it." She folded her arms over her breast and stared defiantly up at him. "Your room must be ready. If it isn't, there are sheets and things down the hall."

He drew an exasperated breath and moved over to the door. "If the bed isn't made up, I'll be back to share yours."

"Is that a threat or a promise?" she asked, trying to sound as if she didn't care either way.

"Neither one. You were the one who wanted company," he reminded her. "I'm just telling you that you're apt to get it."

"In that case, I'll make up another bed down here."

He shrugged. "That's your privilege. At this time of night, I don't intend to play games. If you want me—" He paused to give her a cool look that took in her wrinkled clothes and the appalling pajamas she clutched in her hand. "If you need me for anything," he substituted deliberately, "give a shout."

Kim bit down on her lip hard, aware that she wouldn't ask for help if Jack the Ripper came down the hall dragging Lizzie Borden behind him. "Thank you very much," she managed to say just as coolly. "I'll remember that."

The only satisfaction from that encounter was the door banging behind him so hard that it rattled on the hinges. Even that triumph didn't last long when she realized that there'd be one more repair job on the Stratford's long list.

After she'd gotten into her pajamas and crawled between the icy sheets, the disappointments and frustrations of the day couldn't be subdued any longer. Tears started running down her cheeks, and she turned her head into the pillow so that Gray couldn't hear her crying—although she was sure he wouldn't come calling even if he did.

If he'd evinced the slightest interest—hinted that taking off her clothes might be a pleasure instead of a chore, recognized that she was a woman and not an unattractive one at that—their wedding night might have finished differently.

She really couldn't blame him for losing his temper after her flare-up. Not only that, she'd known that there wasn't any chance he'd find a bare bed in his room and come back to make good his threat. Ozzie's niece came in daily for maid service and would never have left a bed unchanged.

Kim sniffed miserably, then sat up against her pillows to blow her nose. There wasn't any use even trying to rationalize the situation; everything that had happened was a flat-out failure. And tomorrow she'd be back to where it had all started a weekend—no, a lifetime—before.

Chapter Nine

Spring sunlight was dappling the brick wall of her bedroom when Kim awoke the next morning.

A glance at her bedside clock showed that it was the middle of the morning and there certainly wasn't any time to wallow in self-pity. She didn't linger before heading for the shower and later donning a turquoise linen shirtwaist that was a favorite of hers.

It was a good compromise, she decided. She couldn't face her usual working attire of worn slacks and blouse. On the other hand, she'd be darned if she'd wear anything that Gray or Carola might think she'd put on to impress them.

Once she'd slipped into a pair of navy-blue pumps and found a long strand of lapis beads to soften the tailored neckline, she paused next to the wall she shared with Gray's bedroom.

There wasn't the slightest sound from the other side, and she frowned again as she walked back to her door. She'd had thoughts about fixing a really good breakfast, but it looked as if her timing was off again.

To make sure, she went out in the corridor to rap on his bedroom door and then opened it cautiously. The bedroom was empty, but the bed linen was tossed back and his open suitcase rested on a luggage rack. At least he hadn't been so mad that he'd left town at the crack of dawn.

When she got up to the kitchen, she found his breakfast dishes washed and draining on the counter with still-warm coffee in the electric pot. She poured herself a cup and sipped it as she looked around vainly for any kind of a note. Her search took in the living room and the desk by the front door, but without any luck. Apparently Gray didn't plan to leave a paper trail listing his comings and goings just because he'd put his name on a marriage license.

"Damn!" Kim said softly to herself and then went back into the kitchen to pick up the phone extension there.

The floor nurse at the hospital was cautiously optimistic with the latest news of Ozzie. "We're having a hard time keeping him here," she reported cheerfully when Kim identified herself. "He'll be glad to know that you're back home again; he's been worried about leaving the inn without anyone in charge. Can I report that everything's been taken care of so he can relax?"

"I wish you would," Kim said. "All he has to do now is get well. Tell him that I've got a month's work lined up when he comes back."

"I'll do that. Probably that'll help as much as our pills," the nurse replied candidly.

"What about visiting?"

"Wait another day and then check with me again. And Mrs. Stanton," the woman said then before Kim could hang up, "one more thing. I'm sure that Ozzie would want to thank you for that gorgeous plant your husband brought this morning."

"You mean he visited him?"

"No, not really. He knew Ozzie wasn't having any company, but thought he'd enjoy some flowers. And he did."

"I'm glad," Kim said faintly. "Thanks for telling me."

After she'd hung up, she sat staring at the receiver. Gray must have paid a visit to the florist as soon as the shop opened. It was a thoughtful gesture and showed how nice he could be under ordinary circumstances. A temporary wife who snarled at him in the middle of the night couldn't expect anything in return.

As Kim fixed a piece of toast to go with another cup of coffee, she decided to call the Elders back to take over management of the inn as soon as possible. Once Gray left to go south again, she couldn't stay in Port Lathrop and answer questions about her missing husband. She'd go back to her regular job and tell her boss that she didn't need the leave of absence after all. And when it came time for the annulment, Gray's lawyer could get in touch with hers. That decision was enough to make her give the slice of cold toast an unhappy look and finally throw it in the garbage.

The sound of the doorbell came then, and she brushed the crumbs from her fingers as she went to the front door. All of the cautions Gray had taken the night before made her peer through the diamond-shaped glass panes and then smile in relief as she beheld John Amherst's portly figure.

"Come in," she said, swinging the door open. "I'm glad to see a familiar face. Have you had breakfast?"

"Quite a while ago," he told her, "but I wouldn't say no to some coffee if there's any around."

"Of course there is." She gestured toward the living room. "I'll bring it in—"

"There's no need for that. I'm quite accustomed to drinking coffee in the kitchen. You can tell me all about that honeymoon of yours."

"Well, it wasn't long enough," she said, managing to keep her tone light and uncaring. "And you can't run far enough to get away from bad news."

"So I gather." He shook his head as he held the swinging door for her and then followed her into the big kitchen. "That was a terrible thing to happen here. At least Ozzie is doing well."

"I know. I just phoned the hospital." Kim opened the cupboard to find a cup and saucer. "Is there any hope that he can identify who hit him?"

"No one is talking," Amherst said, carefully brushing off the top of a kitchen stool before subsiding on it. "The police chief is more accustomed to overtime parking than assault charges. He's being careful not to say anything that would give it away."

Kim smiled slightly as she took his coffee over to him, thinking how incongruous he appeared in his neat business suit. And then as she put the cup and saucer on the counter at his elbow, she noticed that the morning sunlight made him look every one of his years. It seemed a strange time to realize it—for so long he had simply been Gerald's father, without any real identity. But suddenly in that uncompromising light he looked almost frail. "Let me fix you some toast," she urged the prominent banker. "That will give me an excuse to join you."

"No, thank you. But don't let me stop you," he said politely. "When did you get back?"

"In the middle of the night," she said, debating another piece of toast and then deciding against it, topping her coffee mug instead. "I'm sorry that Gray isn't here—" She broke off when Amherst shook his head at her words.

"I didn't expect him to be here. Not after seeing him downtown a while ago with that nice-looking friend of his. Carola, isn't it?"

"Carola?" Kim's lips parted in astonishment before firming in an unhappy line. It was bad enough that Gray had gone out without saying anything or leaving a note, but to learn that Carola was the reason for his hasty departure was even more galling.

"Why, yes," Amherst was going on innocently. "They were walking down Main Street when I saw them. Having quite a serious discussion," he added, after noting Kim's set expression. "I imagine it was about family affairs—or something like that. Probably she wanted some advice, since your husband is such a new bridegroom," he added, with a heavy-handed attempt at humor. "And that reminds me," he said, reaching for a notebook in his coat pocket. "I must check with him about our tour."

"Tour?"

"Of the port facilities. We'd set up a tentative appointment earlier. Of course, learning about your marriage changed all that," Amherst said, putting his memo book back in his pocket after jotting a reminder in it.

Kim smiled and rubbed at a smudge on the chrome edging of the refrigerator. She wrested her mind back from visions of Gray and Carola with their heads together somewhere downtown and reached for the coffeepot again. "Won't you have some more?"

"No—no, thank you. One cup is plenty. You're probably wondering why I've come calling so early."

"I'm delighted to have some company," she began when the phone rang at the other side of the kitchen. "Excuse me a minute. This shouldn't take long," she assured him, as she reached for the receiver. "We haven't had any guests all week." She altered her tone then to say, "Stratford Inn, good morning."

"Kim? Is that you?"

Gray's voice over the phone made her pulse rocket, and it was an effort for her to respond calmly. "I'm surprised to hear from you. I thought you'd be too busy to call."

"Where did you get that idea?"

"Well, John's here having coffee with me and mentioned he'd seen you downtown earlier."

"John Amherst?" There was a pause before Gray said, "I didn't know you had company. Is he standing in for Gerald today?"

"I haven't any idea." Kim found it was an effort to sound briskly impersonal. Especially when all she wanted to ask was why he was squiring Scott's fiancée around town when he had a perfectly good wife a few blocks away. She forced herself back to grim reality, saying, "Was there something special you wanted?"

Her tone wasn't designed to win any friends, and it didn't. Gray abandoned his attempt at casual conversation as he replied forcefully. "I want you to join me in town. Right away, if possible. There's some business we need to get settled—"

"I can't make it right now," Kim flared, not letting

him finish. "We can do it later, if it's really necessary."

"Later won't do—"

"It'll have to," she cut in again and hung up before he could argue about it. Her knuckles were white as she shoved the phone away, realizing that it was useless to postpone a discussion of her marriage with Gray, but unable to face it with Carola looking on.

"My dear, I hope that I didn't bring on a first quarrel between you two."

Kim looked up to find John staring across at her, a perturbed expression on his face. She managed a travesty of a smile as she came back to pick up her coffee mug again and take a sip. "Of course not. It didn't have anything to do with you. Gray just wanted me to meet him downtown and I turned him down."

"Surely not because I was here." He got to his feet, still disturbed to be even vaguely connected with a family disagreement. "I just wanted to check a few more figures in connection with your loan application that I forgot to get earlier. It shouldn't take long and I can stay here until you return if you're uneasy about leaving the inn alone."

"No—really. It isn't important." She went over to get his cup and saucer, putting them in the sink and running water over them. "You go ahead and do whatever investigating you want. Shall I save any coffee for Gerald?"

John paused by the door into the dining room to glance back over his shoulder. "Gerald? I don't quite understand."

Noting the suddenly strained expression on his face, Kim deduced that probably Gerald was still in the doghouse after his alcoholic weekend at Port

Victor. "I thought he might be coming to pick you up or something. He *did* get back, didn't he?"

"You mean from . . ."

"Port Victor. Gray and I saw him up there over the weekend. We didn't speak to him because he was across the room." There was no need to tell his father that Gerald was also so inebriated at the time that he probably wouldn't have remembered anyhow.

"I haven't seen him." The older man's tight jaw showed that he didn't want to talk about his erring son any more than she wanted to discuss her missing husband, Kim thought wryly. Which only left the weather as a safe topic, or the chances of getting her loan through the bank. And she didn't want to linger on the latter in case that news was bad, too.

She managed a smile as she pushed open the kitchen door. "Isn't it wonderful to finally have a sunny day? I'd better get to work."

Amherst insisted on holding the door so that she could go on through. "Are you coming upstairs, too?"

She thought for a moment and then shook her head. "No, there's a smoke alarm in the basement that needs a battery or the fire department will be issuing a citation on its next inspection. That's my first priority. Do you need a measuring tape? Yardstick? Anything like that?"

He shook his head and patted his coat pocket. "It's an estimate that I'm after. Most of the measurements are in my book already."

"Then I'll leave you to it," Kim said, knowing that if she had to make small talk much longer, she'd disgrace herself by breaking into tears in front of him. And sympathy—even courtly, old-fashioned sympathy—was more than she could handle just then.

The phone rang again before she'd reached the basement stairs. She hesitated, suspecting that Gray might be calling back. She went reluctantly to pick up the receiver, but her voice was haughty as she announced. "This is the Stratford Inn at Port Lathrop."

"Kim? Is that you?"

It was a familiar feminine voice, and Kim sagged against the counter in relief. Her "Hello, Emma—is it that time again?" was in a considerably warmer tone.

The head of the town's Antiquarian League and president of the yearly fund-raiser conceded it was that time indeed. "I hate to ask if the Stratford can be the hostess house again this year, but none of the other places on the tour are in good enough condition."

"It doesn't matter." Considering what else was going on in her life, Kim thought that was true enough. Serving tea to the hundred or so visitors who bought tickets to the Port Lathrop Victorian Homes Tour wasn't a major problem.

"Actually, I think we have enough in our treasury so that the league can help you with the expense," Emma said earnestly.

"Don't worry—the Stratford budget is in better shape than usual," Kim said, crossing her fingers behind her skirt. "A few cups of tea won't sink us."

"That's wonderful. The girls will provide the cookies, as usual."

Kim grinned, aware that most of Emma's "girls" were in their seventies. They also made the best cookies that she'd ever tasted. "Only one thing," she stipulated, "I insist on an extra dozen of those lemon cream delights just for me or I won't play."

"Done," said Emma with relief. "I'll send a letter

along confirming the tour dates and viewing times as soon as we've had our committee meeting. Of course, I suppose it'll be hard to get the girls to talk about anything serious for the next week or so. They'll probably spend most of their time on poor Ozzie Halvorson—he *is* going to be all right, isn't he?"

"The news is good from the hospital this morning."

"Well, that's wonderful! Honestly, the things that have been going on." Emma's voice dropped a notch. "And that Gerald Amherst—wouldn't you think he'd know better?"

Kim blinked in surprise. The Port Lathrop tom-toms hadn't been slow to spread the news again, she thought. Poor Gerald, he wasn't even allowed to have a hangover or a lost weekend in Port Victor without the entire population knowing about it. No wonder his father looked haggard; he'd probably had to endure knowing looks all along Main Street earlier.

"Kim, are you still there?" Emma sounded querulous.

"Yes, of course. I'm sorry—I thought I heard someone," Kim said, trying to think of a plausible excuse to get off the phone before Emma mentioned her sudden swing into matrimony. "The front doorbell only works half the time," she added, using an old fib but a good one.

"I'll let you go then, Kim dear. We'll be in touch soon."

Kim hung up, and wished suddenly for the anonymity of a larger city. Then she thought of all the townspeople whose only vice was an inordinate interest in their neighbors and concluded the good outweighed the bad.

She started for the basement stairs again, but paused halfway down, remembering that the replacement batteries were stored upstairs. Of course, there was a chance Ozzie had replaced the worn-out battery while she'd been in Port Victor. She tried to remember if she'd asked him to and then shook her head. There was only one thing she remembered vividly about that morning, and it was a double bed.

The sound of voices from the neighboring backyard brought her back to reality, and she shook her head irritably. Daydreaming again! And on the basement stairs to boot! Next thing, it would be a padded room.

She went on down to the lower level and inspected the smoke alarm which had altered the course of her life. That worn-out battery on the shelf wasn't the kind of token usually wrapped in a red velvet ribbon, but it might be the only keepsake she'd have out of the whole sorry mess. If she had any pride left, she'd bury the thing in a deep hole with "Rest in peace" as a marker.

At any rate, there weren't any new batteries around, and that meant a trip to the second floor, where she'd have to make small talk with John Amherst again.

She went upstairs and lingered in the empty kitchen, trying to think if there were any jobs to be done on the main floor. At least that was what she rationalized until it became obvious that Gray wasn't going to call back. She started toward the front stairway, telling herself that she'd been a fool to lose her temper when he'd phoned earlier. One more mistake, she reflected, as she trudged up the stairs. It was a pity they didn't give medals for being an idiot, because she'd certainly collected a bushel!

She was so intent on her thoughts that the sound of soft swearing didn't penetrate when she first reached the second-floor landing. Then after identifying John's voice, she wondered what could have roused his wrath. An instant later, her puzzled expression turned to a frown as she decided that he must have fallen and hurt himself during his inspection.

Without hesitating any longer, she went quickly across the carpet, putting an ear to first one door and then hurrying across the big foyer when she concluded the disturbance was coming from her bedroom.

After opening the door, she came to a complete halt as she saw the older man crouched over the big butler's secretary against the far wall. Her eyes widened as the truth sank in—he wasn't inspecting the old bureau; he'd been rifling the desk part. A paper knife still quivered in the wood where he'd been trying to pry open one of the drawers.

"Kim, my dear," he began, taking a hasty step toward her. "I know how this must look, but appearances are deceiving."

"Really." She stared back at him steadily. "Then I wish you'd tell me what's going on. From what I can see, it looks like another kind of breaking and entering. You've been going through my belongings. Or trying to." She moved closer to the desk and surveyed the brass paper knife, frowning as she noticed that it wasn't wedged in a drawer as she'd thought but protruded from the edge of an ornamental wooden pillar next to the drawers.

"Actually I was trying to retrieve something that belonged to Gerald," John said, his voice crisp again. "He forgot to remove it when we sold the secretary to you."

"He also forgot to mention that this thing had any secret compartments," Kim announced when she saw that the paper knife had wedged open the top of the little column, revealing a space behind it. "All you had to do was ask me before you started this treasure hunt," she reproved the older man. "I'm not in the habit of keeping things that don't belong to me."

"I realize that now. It was a mistake—but trying to keep up with Gerald's actions forces me to make them occasionally. I didn't stop to think properly." There was a bitter tinge in his voice as he added, "I'll just collect his property and be on my way. You don't have to worry—I won't damage the wood."

"It's already warped." She watched him as he reached for the knife again. "I imagine that's why the column's sticking."

"If there were more heat in this room, there wouldn't be any trouble," he fumed. "Don't let me keep you from your work."

He so obviously didn't want an onlooker that Kim almost felt sorry for him. Not enough, however, to retreat meekly under his orders. "This is much more interesting than replacing the battery in a smoke alarm," she said, keeping her voice light. "I've always had a hankering for secret compartments. Are there any others in that secretary?"

"Not that Gerald mentioned." Amherst pulled out the brass paper knife and straightened the thin blade before inserting it at the top of the column again.

Kim stood where she was, feeling like an interloper until she realized that, by his deliberate movements, the older man was trying to achieve just that. If she had to stand on one foot and then the other while he fiddled with the warped wood, she'd eventually give up the vigil and leave him to it.

Quite intentionally, she moved still closer to the secretary, leaning against the polished surface.

Amherst turned to give her a hard look. "I hope you can see all right."

"Yes, thanks." She kept her own voice bland. "Can't I give you a hand? I could hold the paper knife while you pry on the top of that column. It looks as if you could get a fingerhold now."

"I can manage, my dear." Amherst straightened again, his patience wearing visibly thin. "Everything would have been so much simpler if you'd married Gerald. Whatever possessed you to throw yourself away on that—that—stranger? His kind will never be happy living in this small town."

"There are more important things than living in Port Lathrop for the rest of my life," she countered and then gave him a baffled glance. "I don't know where you got the idea that I'd ever marry Gerald. We've just been friends all along."

"That isn't what he said. He told me that he expected to propose to you the very day you brought that Stanton fellow to town."

"I didn't *bring* him—" Kim broke off in the middle of her denial when she saw Amherst's bushy gray eyebrows come together. "Gray had to check the port facilities in this part of the world. It was just coincidence that I was in Port Lathrop at the same time. Naturally we were thrilled to be together again."

Her attempt at a bride-like simper must have been successful, because Amherst's thin lips clamped together in disapproval. "Naturally," he said.

She pressed on. "The important thing is that I didn't love Gerald. I'm sorry if he had the wrong idea."

"Love!" Amherst practically spit the word out. "You young fools have no idea of the priorities in life. Do you think you can live happily ever after"—his sarcasm made a travesty of the phrase—"if love is the only thing holding you together? It took me years to convince Gerald that he couldn't expect handouts for the rest of his life. Lasting rewards require planning and patience, but he insisted on taking shortcuts to achieve his ends."

"I really don't see what this has to do with me," Kim began, only to have him cut her off again.

"You'd have meant financial security, and it would have been the making of Gerald. Once he could abandon all of his hare-brained schemes for making money and settle down, his goals would have been different. I've told him so time and time again."

"But I don't have a bean."

Amherst waved her protest aside. "Don't be absurd. You own this inn, and, what's really important, you'll inherit everything from your parents in time. All their property on the peninsula and those acres of timber rights make an impressive estate. Why do you think that the bank even considered a construction loan for this old place?"

"You could have told me," Kim replied, annoyed that her attempt at surviving as a businesswoman hadn't been on her own merits at all. "If I'd known I was such a dandy risk, I would have asked for a bigger loan."

"You haven't gotten the first one yet."

She looked at him with amusement, letting her glance wander to the secretary. "Good Lord, you're not going to try blackmail in addition to everything else!"

He shook his head slowly, as if he'd considered it and already discarded the idea. "No. That isn't my way. Although it might be better for both of us if we forgot this discussion. There's nothing to be gained with the way things are."

"You mean, forget all about that compartment, too?"

He picked up the paper knife and jabbed it next to the column again, as he said, "Obviously that's impossible. Since Gerald isn't around to finish this job, I've been elected." He managed to get a finger in the top of the compartment and yanked forcefully. "That's doing the trick," he grunted, as the wooden section moved a little more.

Kim was still sifting his words. "You mean that Gerald was up here recently trying to retrieve this—this whatever-it-is?" She frowned when Amherst didn't bother to answer, his intent figure hunched over the desk. "Why couldn't he come today?"

"Because he's busy—ah! That does it!" The last elated comment came when the compartment finally gave way, tilting forward so that a sandwich-sized plastic bag could be seen wedged into the space behind the column.

John Amherst pulled it out and put it quickly in his coat pocket, but not before Kim saw that it contained some sort of white powder.

Her eyes went wider still when she considered the possibilities. "I thought you meant something like jewelry or even gold pieces. Drugs never occurred to me," she murmured in a dazed tone, watching him try to put the empty compartment back. "And you have the nerve to criticize Gerald! How could you do anything like this?"

"Keep your voice down," he snapped. "I'm sorry that you had to involve yourself in our affair, but I'm damned if I intend to broadcast it to the whole town."

"I'm sure of that," she countered, not bothering to hide her sarcasm. "John Amherst, pillar of the community. Port Lathrop's esteemed civic leader and dope dealer on the side. All this time you've been doing the same things you've condemned in others!"

"Don't be ridiculous. I wouldn't jeopardize my health with this stuff." He patted his bulging pocket.

"Then why . . ."

"It was an insurance policy. Gerald's idea again. In case he had to make a sudden retreat. Evidently you didn't hear the morning newscast." Amherst was looking around the room, as if checking to make sure that he hadn't forgotten anything. He picked up the brass paper knife before closing the desk front and hefted it absently, then slipped it in his other coat pocket.

Kim's brows drew together as she watched him, and for the first time a sliver of fear sliced through her consciousness. She took a step backward, trying to remember how close she was to the doorway without actually looking over her shoulder.

As if on a separate plane, she heard her voice asking calmly, "What did the morning newscast have to do with this?"

"There was a police raid at the Haymarket in Victoria early this morning. Since Gerald was a major stockholder of the firm, the authorities want to talk to him, but he doesn't choose to be available at the moment." Amherst moved toward the door beside her, keeping his voice level and unhurried, as if they were discussing the success of Port Lathrop's newest project and not the crackdown on an illicit drug operation just across the border.

"I should think he'd be more interested in proving his innocence. Of course, if he isn't . . ." Her voice trailed off as she thought about it.

"That's the dilemma. Shall we go downstairs?" He waved her ahead of him with one of his courtly gestures.

Kim went through the bedroom doorway into the big second-floor foyer at the head of the old curving stairway which was one of the architectural wonders of the house. It was a steep descent, with narrow carpeted steps and a gracefully curving polished hand-rail leading down to the front door. Countless numbers of Port Lathrop brides had gone down it each season, because it provided a marvelously romantic staging for their gowns of tulle and lace.

Stained-glass windows near the painted ceiling filtered the morning sunlight downward, imposing blotches of blood reds and deep blues on the carpeted steps below. To Kim's glance just then, the blotches brought back a more grisly memory—the patch downstairs where Ozzie's blood still stained the wide oak flooring.

"You go ahead," she told Amherst, trying to cloak her sudden nervousness. "And you don't have to worry about my involving you. Actually, I don't know anything except for . . ."

"My insurance?" He patted his pocket again, as if reassuring himself that he still possessed the packet from the desk. "Unfortunately, you still make it awkward for me, my dear. You see, without your testimony there's nothing to connect me with Gerald's misfortunes. Even his business associates"—a wintry smile came over Amherst's face for an instant and then disappeared again—"can't furnish any proof. And there's too much money involved for me to leave loose ends."

Kim dug her heels into the carpet, trying to resist the unrelenting pressure of his hand in the middle of her back as they moved toward the head of the stairway. "Ozzie's another loose end," she pointed out, desperately trying to delay and distract him. "And he's getting better. The hospital said so this morning."

"That old fool doesn't know what hit him. It was so dark that he can't possibly identify anybody. And there's no reason for him to connect Gerald or me with the break-in. If Carola hadn't decided to spend the weekend here while you were gone, I could have collected Gerald's package and you needn't have been in the middle of this. I'm sorry, Kim." For an instant, there was a look in his eyes that brought back the family friend she'd known for so long, and then it faded to an impersonal glaze as he maneuvered her to the top of the stairs. "At least this will be quick."

His hands came out in a lightning gesture, as if he planned to shove her down the steep stairs. Kim whirled to clutch the shiny waxed banister, fighting desperately to keep her balance.

Then he launched himself upon her, and she discovered that he wasn't risking her chance of survival in a fall down those steps—the man was trying to push her over the railing, a plunge of more than thirty feet, onto the entranceway below. As Kim struggled frantically to hang on to the slippery balustrade, Amherst was using his greater strength to pull her fingers away. "You're just making it harder," he gritted out. "Like that damned Ozzie. But you won't get away the way he did. Stop that! You rotten little . . ."

He hit her savagely with the back of his hand after she bit him and then grunted in triumph as she sagged, momentarily stunned by the force of the blow.

Kim felt his fingers close on her throat, and her struggles grew weaker as his grip tightened. She could hear wheezing and knew that it was her own breath rasping in her ears. Darkness hovered on the edge of her consciousness in her final futile effort against Amherst's attack. It was no use—there wasn't a chance—she couldn't fight any longer, and his shouted curse confirmed it.

Then, like a miracle, the pain was gone. Kim was vaguely aware that she'd slumped onto the stairs and that someone was holding her there so that her dazed body didn't slither on down the steep steps.

She took a deep, hurting breath and, after recognizing Gray's anxious face as he bent over her, sagged into his arms. Just as if there weren't a big Port Lathrop policeman looking benevolently down on them after he slipped a pair of handcuffs on John Amherst.

"Are you all right now, Mrs. Stanton?" the officer asked. "I can put in a call for the medics."

Kim drew back reluctantly from Gray's clasp, leaning against the hard wooden newel post as she tested the skin on her bruised throat. "I'll be all right," she whispered. And then in a louder tone, "Just give me a minute or two."

"You have all the time in the world. Amherst here"—the policeman jerked a thumb at the older man—"isn't going anywhere except downtown. Even a good lawyer won't get him out after a homicide attempt."

"I have an idea that it was two attempted homicides," Gray put in without taking his gaze from Kim's face. He got to his feet then and pulled her carefully up beside him. "Time will tell on that."

"You'd better take that package from his coat pocket," Kim added, keeping her glance averted from John Amherst's stony one. "It was the reason that he came here in the first place."

The policeman whistled as he saw the contents of the plastic envelope, and then his expression hardened as he glanced at the man beside him. "Even two or three lawyers won't do anything for you if we can make this charge stick. You'd better take a good deep breath when you get outside, because it might be the last one for a long spell." He marched his captive down the narrow steps, keeping a careful grasp on him all the while. When they were halfway, the officer looked up at Gray and Kim, still standing quietly at the top of the stairs. "We'll need a statement from both of you."

Kim nodded and Gray said, "You'll get it. Maybe a little later, if that's okay."

"Sure thing." The policeman surveyed Kim's pale face with concern. "Is everything under control here?"

Gray put a strong arm around her shoulders. "If it isn't," he replied in an ominous tone, "it soon will be."

Chapter Ten

Kim girded herself for a verbal attack after the front door closed behind Amherst and his captor, but Gray merely kept a firm grip on her elbow and steered her down the back stairs.

"I imagine you've had enough of that other view," he commented roughly as they made their way to the kitchen. "For a minute there, I thought we'd left it too late."

"So did I." She brushed her hair back with fingers that still trembled and stared up at him as he pushed open the big swinging door for her. "I wish I'd known you were on the way—I didn't have the foggiest idea."

"You hung up before I could mention it," Gray said grimly. He ushered her onto a low stool before going over to the sink to fill the kettle. "Hot tea comes first. Afterward, I'll take you to the hospital emergency room. You need somebody to look at that throat."

His analytical tone didn't help her morale, and Kim wondered if she'd imagined the way he'd held her at the top of the stairs such a short time ago. Of course, she reminded herself unhappily, there wasn't much else the poor man could do after she'd launched herself at him like a berserk missile.

"I'll be fine," she insisted, realizing that it was true. She'd be black and blue, but that was all. There was no use dwelling on her other hurts. "What made you come rushing to my rescue?" she asked, trying to sound casual about it.

"After I heard the newscast on Gerald's disappearance, I told the police about seeing him at the Haymarket over the weekend. Apparently the Canadian authorities suspected drug involvement on both sides of the border. They thought that Amherst's connection at the port might play a part in the dope pipeline from the Far East, so it wasn't only Gerald they wanted to contact. I was at the police station when I called and you said John was here. We didn't waste any time on the way. Thank God!"

Kim nodded soberly and watched him pour boiling water over tea bags in the two mugs he'd gotten out. "I must have been the only person in Port Lathrop who missed the morning news. All the talk about Gerald didn't sink in. John was taking a risk, though."

"By then he didn't have anything to lose." Gray handed her a mug of tea and went over to perch on another stool with his. "Probably he planned to get in touch with Gerald later, and he couldn't afford to leave the packet around."

Kim took a sip of tea, wincing when she swallowed the hot liquid. "That stuff must have been worth thousands. 'Insurance' was what John called it."

"I've heard a lot of other descriptions that fitted it better. When you think of the hell the drug scene causes—" Gray broke off, shaking his head. "Hurry up and drink your tea. We should get going."

"I tell you I don't need to see a doctor."

His face settled in a familiar determined expression.

"I don't intend to argue about it. I'm taking you downtown for someone to check you over. After that, if everything's all right you can come back here and rest or wash windows or dance the Highland Fling for the rest of the day."

She was watching him carefully over the top of her tea mug. "You won't be around to object?"

"Not this afternoon. I've had to make other plans." He sighed and put his empty mug down on the edge of the sink beside him, kneading the muscles at the back of his neck.

Kim noticed the tired lines at the corners of his eyes as the sunlight filtered through the kitchen curtain. "I forgot about Carola," she said dully, draining her own mug into the sink. "John told me he saw you with her this morning."

She was turned away from him, so she didn't see Gray's jaw harden, as if he'd been goaded to the limit. "I'm surprised that we missed making the newscast as a top story. Did Amherst mention that Carola plans to drive south today—if everything works out?" he asked.

"No, he didn't." Gray's terse report made Kim's cheeks go even whiter. She looked around to find her purse wedged against the canister on the counter and picked it up carefully. "I can't blame Carola for being tired of Port Lathrop. Will she be coming back to the inn first?"

"I didn't recommend it. Let's go, shall we?" He walked over to hold the kitchen door. "Do you need a sweater?"

"I have one in the front hall."

"Then we'll pick it up on the way."

The next hour or so followed the same impersonal

yet polite course. Gray waited in the emergency section of the hospital and nodded approvingly when the doctor emerged with her to say that she'd suffer discomfort from the bruising but there was no serious damage. The physician also recommended that she get some rest after her ordeal and sent along an envelope with a few yellow pills to help her sleep.

"You'd better take one this afternoon," Gray told Kim as he drove her to the police station afterward. "The way you look now, I'm surprised that they didn't insist on your staying in the hospital overnight."

Kim refrained from admitting that the doctor had suggested just that. "I'll be fine," she said levelly. "Let's hope that the police haven't had second thoughts about my part in all this."

"Why should they?" Gray asked, pulling up in front of the building.

"They might think Gerald hid other stuff in secret compartments at the inn while he was about it. Besides that cranny in the butler's secretary."

"Are there any other hiding places?" Gray asked with a sudden frown.

She managed a thin smile. "There's a mousehole down in the storage room. I'm surprised you didn't notice it when you disconnected that smoke alarm. Oh, damn!"

He paused in the midst of opening his car door. "Now what's wrong?"

"I just remembered that I forgot to replace that battery this morning—I was on my way to do it when I got sidetracked on the second floor."

"Don't worry about that," Gray said, sliding out of the car. "I'll fix it when I drive you back to the inn. Let's get this statement over with first, and with any luck we'll have time to stop for a sandwich afterward."

The depositions were a straightforward affair, but Kim saw Gray give an anxious look at his watch when they emerged from the police headquarters afterward.

Before he could mention the time, Kim managed to yawn and say, "I think I'll skip lunch after all. Could you just drive back to the inn, please?"

"Of course." Gray kept his voice noncommittal, but there was no hiding the relief on his face. "I'll get you settled and then be on my way."

To join Carola, Kim thought as she settled dejectedly back against the seat. At least she could find out for sure. "Will you be coming back to the inn later?"

"Naturally." Gray shot her a frowning glance before pulling onto the main street. The he spoiled it by adding, "I'm not sure about dinner. There's no way I can tell now. Don't count on it. Can you manage something to eat?"

"Heavens, yes." There was no reason for him to feel that he had to be responsible for her every move until he finally left town, Kim thought. "After I have a nap, I'll be perfectly fine."

Gray insisted that she swallow one of the prescribed yellow pills when they finally got back to the inn. Afterward, he made sure that she was resting on top of her bed before he left and announced that he'd have the next-door neighbors check on her during the afternoon. Since Kim had gravitated to the basement bedroom again, she agreed to the baby-sitting scheme. At least it would be easy for them to look in, and since the yellow pill was taking effect by then, she found it was too much effort to argue. She fell asleep while Gray was still pulling a light cover up over her feet.

Either the pill was stronger than she'd imagined or her physical reaction to the morning's high drama was more pronounced. Whatever the cause, Kim's deep slumber lasted almost until dinner. She awakened then, stiff and unbelieving, as she checked the clock on her bedside table.

A peek into the bedroom next door disclosed that true to his word, Gray hadn't returned in time for dinner. Kim grimaced and decided to find something in the kitchen to compensate for missing lunch.

She would have had an omelet except that even the sight of an egg brought back memories she'd rather forget. She settled instead for a grilled cheese sandwich and listened to the local news on the radio as she ate. There was a veiled reference to "important local figures" involved in an international drug arrest, and Kim reached over to turn off the radio before she heard any more.

She rinsed out her empty milk glass and tidied the kitchen counter before wandering down to the basement level again. A quick look in the storage room showed that Gray had evidently changed the smoke alarm battery as he had promised, so she didn't even have that job left.

By then, she'd become reconciled to the probability that Gray wouldn't be back until late. There was no use wandering around to wait up for him, because she really didn't want to hear what he'd been doing all afternoon and evening. There'd be time enough in the morning for him to explain politely that he couldn't hang around Port Lathrop any longer now that she'd recovered and give her his business address or the name of his attorney.

Kim thrust that thought from her and decided to take a warm bath before going back to bed. She made it last as long as possible and felt slightly more cheerful when she emerged from the scented hot water. Cheerful enough to search out her new blue nightgown and put it on after she'd toweled herself dry. Her reflection in the mirror raised her spirits still more, and she was smiling as she went back in the bedroom and slid into bed. It was a pity that the heating of the Stratford lent itself more to flannel than flimsy, but at least she could pretend otherwise.

She fell asleep on that pleasant fantasy, and when there was a noise in the hall later, she automatically decided that it was part of the dream. It wasn't until after she heard her bedroom door open slightly and became conscious of light from the corridor that she stirred and tried to come back to reality.

By the time she opened her eyes and sat up, the door was closed again. She heard footsteps going into Gray's room and his own door shut softly. Kim fumbled for the light and said a fervent "Damn" when the clock showed it was just after ten.

She chewed on her lip as she sat there, debating whether to go and knock on Gray's bedroom door. The trouble was, she needed a logical excuse. She couldn't appear in her negligee and offer to cook him a late snack—not with her culinary reputation! And she certainly didn't have the right to barge in and ask what he'd been doing all day. Or more to the point, who he'd been doing it with. Or was it whom?

Anyway, it was a lost cause. Kim sighed as she acknowledged it and reached across to turn off the light again. She lay back and then readjusted her pillow, wondering why it suddenly felt as if it were stuffed with glass floats from the waterfront.

The minutes dragged by endlessly. Fully thirty of them had gone by according to the illuminated dial on her alarm clock before her eyelids started to grow heavy. She'd blinked twice and yawned once when a sudden blare of sound brought her upright as if she'd been poked with a sharp stick. She started to turn on the bedside lamp when the raucous noise sounded from down the hall again. It was so unnerving that she knocked the lampshade askew, managing to drag the alarm clock off the table in the process.

By the time the third blaring came down the hall, she'd identified it and was halfway out her bedroom door, dragging on her negligee as she went. She winced as her bare feet came into contact with a piece of grit on the floor by the storage-room door, but she didn't let it slow her down.

It would be the final degrading blow if Gray had his sleep interrupted at the Stratford again. He'd be out of the place before sunup if the racket continued.

That despairing thought was going through Kim's mind as she flipped on the storage-room light. She dragged a box hastily over to the far wall so that she could reach the alarm, where a red plastic flag on the side confirmed that the battery was almost gone. As if she didn't know! The box gave another wounded buffalo cry, and she muttered an angry epithet as she clambered up on the box to disconnect the wires. It *would* be her luck to have bought a defective battery!

She ripped the wires free and stared at the alarm with loathing. At least she'd managed to disconnect the thing without Gray's happening on the scene again. She sighed and got down off the box, being careful that the lace on her negligee didn't catch on the rough wood. Tomorrow, she told herself bitterly, she'd go back to pajamas. At least it wouldn't matter if they snagged on anything!

She turned out the light and trudged back up the hall, aware that it would have been smarter if she'd stopped to put on some slippers. She paused for an instant at Gray's bedroom door, and her expression relaxed. The quiet on the other side showed that this time he hadn't been disturbed. Praise heaven for small favors!

When she opened her own bedroom door, it was instantly apparent that she'd celebrated too soon.

"What are you doing here?" she gasped, almost falling over Gray as he straightened from lighting the fire in her bedroom fireplace.

"I came to call, and make sure you'd recovered," he said, helping her keep her balance by putting his hands at her elbows. "You looked so tired earlier that you scared me. Besides, I've decided the Stratford isn't the place to sleep."

"I'm terribly sorry about the noise," she began and then paused as she realized he was still keeping her close even though there was no real need. "And I feel fine." When he didn't relax his grip, she started again. "It was that same smoke alarm. I don't know what happened. That replacement battery you put in must have been defective." When he didn't answer, she looked up at him more closely and discovered his eyes held a fugitive gleam of laughter which she couldn't ignore. Then she noticed for the first time that this certainly was an informal call, since he wasn't wearing anything except a dark-blue dressing gown.

Gray must have been doing a survey of his own, because he nodded approvingly at her satin negligee and then started untying the belt at her waist. "Very nice. Very nice, indeed, but you'd better take it off."

"Take it off?" She stared up at him as he steered her toward the bed.

"That's right. After trotting around these halls, you're beginning to turn the same shade of blue." He pulled back the covers and draped the negligee over the end of the bed, as she obediently crawled between the sheets. They'd turned icy in the interval, and she shivered on contact.

"Still cold?" Gray settled on the edge of the mattress beside her.

"A little." She stared at him warily.

"I *could* help," he said, as if discussing a method of procedure.

Kim took a deep breath then, very much aware of how handsome he looked in the flickering light of the fire. And the warmth wasn't restricted to that side of the room. Her heart was thundering again, and Gray knew it—she could tell by the way his gaze lingered over the frothy lace bodice of her gown and the expanse of soft skin it revealed.

"You made an offer in Port Victor and then changed your mind," she told him, unaware of how lovely she looked as she stared tremulously back. "I'm not sure I like your rules."

He picked up her hand, playing with the tips of her fingers as he confessed, "I don't blame you. Kissing you that night was a mistake. No, don't move away, you idiot," he said roughly when she tried to retreat.

"I really don't want to hear . . ."

"Kissing you was a mistake," he went on, ignoring her interruption, "because I suddenly realized that I didn't want an affair with you." He felt her instinctive withdrawal at that and caught her shoulders to shake her just once. "That was because I suddenly knew that a weekend wasn't long enough—I wanted a lifetime."

"But I thought you hated the idea of getting married."

"A shotgun ceremony wasn't the ideal way of getting to know you, but it was a start. I knew I didn't dare rush you or we'd both regret it in the long run." His hands slowly slid down from her shoulders, and Kim couldn't control her shiver of delight at his caressing touch. Gray's eyes darkened, and he would have pulled her close except that she put a palm against his chest—anxious to clear away the last barrier.

"And that's why you made a fast exit?" she asked.

"Exactly. It seemed like a good idea to put some distance between us."

"So you skipped the country. Fine thing." Her mouth quivered with laughter and relief. Apparently Gray had been suffering pangs all during that weekend, too. "Were you still in retreat today?"

"Hell, no." He rested his head against her hair to add, "Although it may have seemed like it. I pointed Carola south to meet Scott's plane in Seattle. We'll probably have both of them back in a day or so, but we'll have to play that by ear. Maybe they'll want to visit the Game Farm with us when we go calling." He tucked a soft strand of her hair behind her ear and dropped a kiss in that vicinity before adding, "This afternoon I had to tour the whole damned waterfront at Port Victor. Tomorrow I'll do Port Lathrop and submit my report to the main office. It has to be in before I can take time off for a proper honeymoon."

"You mean—all this time today—you've been working?"

"Well, of course." He raised his head to scowl fondly down at her. "What in the hell do you think I was doing?" Seeing her guilty look, he sighed and said, "I suppose I might as well get used to it."

"I'll try to do better."

"Well, you can start right now," Gray said, shedding his robe and pulling back the covers to get in bed beside her. "It's colder than a well-digger's posterior in this place. I expect you to act like a proper Victorian landlady and make me forget it."

Kim quivered again as she felt his long length against her, and it was an effort to ask, "What about Victorian landladies?"

"They had a reputation for being extremely hospitable to the paying guests. And since there's no sleep to be had at the Stratford . . ."

"That's not my fault this time." She caught his hand and stopped its devastating explorations just for an instant. "You put a bad battery in that alarm today—" She broke off then as she felt his shoulders shake with laughter. "You didn't change it at all," she said with sudden certainty, pushing up on an elbow to stare accusingly down at him. "You put the old one back in."

"Well, I had to do something to get us in the same room," he said unrepentantly. He slipped the narrow satin straps of her nightgown off her shoulders with calm assurance and pulled her back down against him once again. "I fell in love with you when I woke up and found you in bed with me that first time, and I've been figuring out how to get us back here ever since."

The laughter faded from his eyes as her fingers feathered a soft trail of their own. He bent to kiss her. Lightly at first and then roughly, like a man starved for possession.

It was much, much later before Kim was able to whisper, "Thank heavens you thought of the battery."

Gray's arm at her waist tightened. "If it hadn't been that, I'd have found something else. You didn't have a prayer of getting away, Mrs. Stanton."

Mrs. Stanton decided she must be the most willing victim since all those Victorian landladies and sensibly pulled her husband closer—so that she could surrender again.

About the Author

Glenna Finley is a native of Washington State. She earned her degree from Stanford University in Russian Studies and in Speech and Dramatic Arts, with emphasis on radio.

After a stint in radio and publicity work in Seattle, she went to New York City to work for NBC as a producer in its international division. In addition, she worked with the "March of Time" and *Life* magazine.

As a producer, she had her own show about activities in Manhattan, a show that was broadcast to England. The programs were similar to those of the "Voice of America."

Though her life in New York was exciting, she eventually returned to the Northwest where she married. Currently residing in Seattle with her husband, Donald Witte, and their son, she loves to travel, and draws heavily on her travels and experiences for the novels that have been published. Her books for NAL have sold several million copies.

⊘

SIGNET Romances by Glenna Finley